NURSE'S DIARY

Romance seems a long way off for Nurse Asta Milne when she first encounters Larry, a doctor lodging next door. She is recovering from a broken engagement to Dick, but wonders if she's been a little too hasty. Asta is offered a job escorting a small girl back to her home in Sydney, only to find that Larry is on the same plane. After a forced landing in the desert, she is forced to change her mind about Larry.

Books by Louie Williams
in the Linford Romance Library:

ONE SPRING AT ST MARGARET'S

LOUIE WILLIAMS

NURSE'S DIARY

Complete and Unabridged

LINFORD
Leicester

First published in Great Britain in 1981 by
Robert Hale Limited
London

First Linford Edition
published 1998
by arrangement with
Robert Hale Limited
London

British Library CIP Data

Williams, Louie
    Nurse's diary.—Large print ed.—
Linford romance library
1. Love stories
2. Large type books
I. Title
823.9'14 [F]

ISBN 0–7089–5249–6

Published by
F. A. Thorpe (Publishing) Ltd.
Anstey, Leicestershire

Set by Words & Graphics Ltd.
Anstey, Leicestershire
Printed and bound in Great Britain by
T. J. International Ltd., Padstow, Cornwall

This book is printed on acid-free paper

1

GLANCING at her watch, Asta Milne hastily returned her diary to the dressing-table drawer, and peeping into the mirror, adjusted the jaunty little tricorne hat. On the front was a monogram in gold letters.

'R.T.M.' it said, standing for 'Rodney Temporary Nursing' but known to the nurses on its register as 'Rent-a-Nurse'.

It was just that, a number of male and female nurses who for various reasons preferred to be freelance, and not connected to a Hospital.

After some eighteen months, Asta still liked the constant change of environment and patients. It meant she was free to take a few days or even weeks off whenever she liked.

Now, on this stunningly bright day in late April, she found herself hoping her next assignment would be somewhere in the country, where her off-duty could be spent in a nice garden, or exploring some quaint village.

A small-featured girl with large blue eyes frowned back at her, and Asta put out the tip of her tongue to the image, pulling the cap down on silky fair hair that had been shampooed last evening and was about as manageable as a stray sunbeam.

Taking a quick look through her bedroom window, her face brightened.

"At last," she called out to her mother, as she ran down the stairs to the kitchen, "I do believe we're going to see some action outside."

She took another look through the kitchen curtains. "Mrs Biggs's lodger has actually taken his hands out of his pockets at last. Now he's walking right up to that car. He's leaning over that horrible man in the purple shirt, Mummy, telling him something. Oh go on, do! Surely you're not afraid of that nasty little — " She gave an infuriated gasp. "No! The stupid idiot's grinning at the man as though it's all a huge joke."

Her pert nose wrinkled disdainfully. "My goodness, I've a jolly good mind to go out there and tell him to move the car myself. This is the third morning running he's blocked our driveway. It's infuriating."

Mrs Milne's bright blue eyes twinkled with amusement. "You sound just as though you're giving a running commentary on a football match, dear," she said, putting the toast rack on the table. "Surely you don't want a fight on our doorstep, Mortimer Road's a very respectable place."

Taking another careful peep through the lemon yellow curtains of the bright kitchen, Asta tried to make out what the two men outside were saying, but could only guess at what was going on. The fat man sitting in a huge gleaming American car was waving his pudgy hands about like a tic-tac man at the races. Obviously he was claiming his right to park the car wherever he chose, even if it did take up most of the frontage of two neat suburban houses.

In other circumstances, Asta's highly developed sense of fun would have found the scene amusing, but it meant she wasn't going to be able to get her Mini out of the garage. Well, not without difficulty, anyway.

Glancing at a Black Forest clock ticking away on the wall, just clearing its throat in preparation for announcing the demise of another hour, she gave a little gesture of annoyance. "I'm going to be in time to catch all the traffic again."

Nibbling a piece of toast, however, she was drawn irresistibly back to the window.

"Do come away from there," said her mother, "they'll see you. There's no point in getting involved."

Mrs Milne was a mature version of her only daughter. Oval-faced, with a firm chin and fine bones, yet with a lack of perfect symmetry that added interest to the discerning eye. Lively blue eyes set wide apart, and glossy hair a few shades darker than Asta's. A neat five feet of body structure that made even the blue house smock she wore look smart enough for a party.

"I'm quite sure the boy next door is capable of fighting his own battles," she said, mildly. "Time *is* getting along, dear, and I do worry about your driving through all that traffic, especially when you're in a hurry."

Shrugging her slim shoulders, Asta said "I'm late now, anyway. I expect all the best jobs will have been allocated. Mrs Adams has been very good, finding me day-time shifts near home, but I can't expect her to go on doing it now you're well again."

Giving one more peep through the curtains she said "With that fiery red hair you'd think the man next door would be more belligerent, wouldn't you? He ought to stand up for his rights."

"I wouldn't call his hair exactly fiery, Asta, it's a nice shade of auburn, I think. I rather imagine it's *your* rights he's standing up for, too. He doesn't usually take his own car out so early as this."

"Then he needn't bother," came the indignant reply. "I'm capable of standing up for myself, thank you. I certainly don't need his help."

She took an appraising look at the tall figure outside in the road, whose skin must have been tanned by a fiercer sun than one usually got in England. He stood squarely in the space being disputed, one hand thrust into the pocket of a pair of disreputable jeans, showing every sign of being on intimate terms with the engine of an elderly Ford parked nearby.

"I think it's sweet of the boy to take the trouble," said Mrs Milne, firmly. "I did happen to mention to Mrs Biggs, next door, what a job you had the other morning getting your car out with that big one parked so close. She must have mentioned it to him."

"He's not making much of a success,"

said Asta, dryly. "Old purple-shirt shows no sign of turning away."

She watched a shaft of sun light up the younger man's crisply curling hair as he stood, complacently nodding at the other's heated remarks. He was a lot older than she had thought at first. There was a distinct spattering of white by his ears. But for that he might have passed for a mere boy.

"I just can't bear to see someone like that bombastic bully get away with it, that's all," she said, stormily. "He needs someone to stand up to him. Just look at him now, actually brandishing his fist. The man next door must be twice his size. Well, twice as tall, anyway."

Her eyes bright with indignation, Asta said "What idiots some men are. If it wasn't so late I'd phone the police and complain of his causing an obstruction. They'll be having to call an ambulance to that lobster-faced man soon. He's practically frothing at the mouth. Next thing you know he'll be needing my attention. I sometimes think the 'minist'ring angel' stuff can be overdone. It wouldn't surprise me one bit if that idiotic red-haired man doesn't end up moving his own car to make room for that . . . that petrol-eater."

"Better let them have a few more minutes to settle the argument, dear. As you said, you're late anyway. There's another cup of coffee in the pot if you'd like it?"

"Thanks Mummy, perhaps I will. I don't suppose that awful man in the car even lives in this road," she said. "Why doesn't he park outside his own house? Probably keeps *another* car there."

Tossing her head, Asta took the cup of coffee her mother poured out. Catching sight of her own angry face reflected in a mirror over the fireplace made her realise she had been taking life a little too seriously of late. There was a distinct worry line between her delicately pencilled brows. Her mother was right. It was stupid to allow herself to get involved with what was going on outside. She knew she'd been a bit tetchy recently, not sleeping too well since breaking off her engagement to Dick. That, combined with coping with a complaining woman patient who'd kept her on her feet all day for the past few weeks. Thank goodness that job was over.

Mrs Milne finished putting the blue and white spotted breakfast cups back on the dark oak old Welsh dresser, and rubbed a dab of cream into her well-kept hands. The women of her family had always been known for their beautiful hands, and Asta's, slim, long-fingered, were no exception, although her work as a nurse made her keep the nails well-trimmed.

"It's an old wives' tale that red hair always goes with a fiery temper, anyway," she said. "Mrs Biggs caught me out in the garden the other day. She's a very good-hearted woman, but once she starts talking it's very hard to get away. Poor soul, she must be lonely at times, I suppose. Can you imagine her in the front row of the chorus? She showed me a photograph. It seems incredible when you see her now. It was that lovely sunny morning last week, and I was putting in some wallflower plants. She says Larry is the best boarder she ever had. Gives her no trouble at all, which is more than you could say for some of the students she's had, since Mr Biggs died. Do you remember the one with the drum kit, who played until the early hours? And that hairy monster who was caught leaning over the fence to look into our bathroom?"

"Isn't this one a bit old for a student?" asked Asta. "He looks well over thirty, I'd think. Quite old enough to stand up for himself, anyway."

"Thirty-one, a nice age for a man, I think. Mature, but not *too* old. Such a friendly smile he has. He insisted on carrying my shopping home when I met him in the High Street yesterday. He's writing a thesis, I hear, and doing a part-time refresher course at St Margaret's hospital, where you trained."

Her eyebrows now two question marks, Asta asked "A Doctor, is he? You'd never guess it in those clothes. And how do you know his age? Surely you didn't *ask* him? Really, Mummy."

"Mrs Biggs told me he brought home a bottle of wine and a cake one evening quite recently. He said it was his birthday, and asked her to share them." She gave a sigh. "Poor man, it seems so sad to have no one to spend your birthday with but a landlady. I'd have asked him in here for a meal if I'd known!"

"Really, Mummy," Asta said again, then her tone softened. "It's a pity we don't live in a castle, you'd have made a wonderful Lady Bountiful. You'd turn this house into another Doctor Barnardo's if you had your way, taking in all the lame dogs."

"Wouldn't the Battersea Dog's Home

11

be more appropriate?" asked her mother, smiling at the idea. "He really is rather a lamb, though. I'm sure Mrs Biggs feeds him enough, but she's more than a little lacking in mental nourishment, and he must miss his home life. He comes from Sydney, you know, dear. A place called Wooloomaloo, or something that sounds like that." She rolled the name around her tongue again. "Fascinating names they have in Australia, don't they? Aborigine, he told me."

"I hate lambs, especially the male variety," said Asta, with a sniff. "The world's too full of sheep already. I prefer a man who can utter a decisive 'Bah!' than a weak 'baaah'. Most women still like a man they can look up to, no matter what the 'libbers' may say."

The laughter lines around her mother's lustrous eyes deepened. "Larry must be all of six feet, dear. I doubt if you come up to his shoulder. He has a pretty good physique, too. I've noticed him in Mrs Biggs's garden, stripped to the waist to do some digging for her. Quite impressive, I assure you. I prefer to talk to him when he's sitting, he makes my neck ache looking up at him otherwise."

She surveyed her daughter's slim figure in its smart navy blue uniform coat. "Yes, just about up to his shoulder, I'd say."

"You can look up to a man who's five feet two, so long as he's made of the right stuff," said Asta, a little impatiently. "But you know perfectly well what I mean. You seem to have made friends with him terribly quickly."

"Larry came in and mended that hall plug for me. I've been trying to get someone to do it for ages. Electricians don't seem to want to know unless you need the whole house rewired. Naturally I gave him a coffee, and he sat in the kitchen and talked to me for a while. No doubt he was just being polite to an older woman, but not every man bothers these days.

He's quite shattered any previous ideas I might have had about Australians being a little — well — uncouth."

"Larry!" said Asta, scornfully, "even his name sounds like a lamb. It suits him, I should think. *I've* always thought of Australian men as great tough husky ones who could stand up for themselves against anyone. On all the films I've seen they've been shown as giants wielding axes. Judging from his performance out there with that ghastly man in the car, he'd be more at home with a pencil sharpener."

"Aren't you being a little unkind, dear? He need not have gone out to speak to the man at all, you know. *I* like Larry very much, even if he does appear to have made a poor impression on you. Just because he's not brawling with that man in the street, it doesn't make him a coward, you know."

"Why you had to get on first name terms with someone I've been trying to avoid ever since he came to live next door, I don't know. *I'm* not collecting lost sheep, even if you are, Mummy. Oh sorry! I'm a bit cross this morning. You must have been glad of his help, I'm sure. Only don't try to get me involved."

"His name is really Laurence," came her mother's reply. "I rather like it myself. If you'd been ringing every electrician within miles without getting any response, you'd know how grateful I was for Larry's help. I just happened to mention my problem to Mrs Biggs, and she must have told Larry, for he was round here the next evening, complete with fuse-wire and screwdriver. Then we sat talking. I was glad of his company."

"What ever did you find to talk about?" asked Asta, endeavouring to look interested. She knew she'd been a bit terse with her mother, and was a little ashamed.

"Gardening mostly. He's taken over the garden next door. You remember what a state it was in since Mr Biggs died? He's coming in this evening, as a matter of fact, to see to the iron. You know how hot it gets. If I take it to the shop they'll keep it for weeks, or else some snooty young man will say 'of course, Madam, this iron has had its day, hasn't it? It would pay you to buy a new one.' They don't seem to be interested in mending anything these days."

"It's very kind of him," conceded Asta, "I shall be spending the evening with Brenda. You know she's looking for a new flat? Don't bother with supper for me, Mummy, we'll probably have a meal out."

Kissing her mother's proffered cheek, she said "I must go. I hope they'll be sending me out on a maternity case, or something. It would be a doddle after my last month with that cantankerous old lady."

"Jim will be round later," her mother said. "I expect Larry will have finished by then. I've promised to give a hand with the costumes for the drama club. They want me to play the part of

16

Gretel, in 'White Horse Inn', but I'm much too old for it."

"Nonsense," said Asta, warmly. "You don't look a day over thirty, and you know it. Make-up can work marvels for the stage."

"Thank you dear," answered her mother, a trifle wryly. "Jim seems to think so, even off the stage."

Asta took a swift glance at the reddened cheeks. Well well! No time to pursue that line just now. No one can stop the thoughts rushing through their brain, just the same. In the short space of time between closing the kitchen door, tapping across the hall, and nearly falling over a threadbare patch in the carpet, Asta had plenty of time to reflect.

She'd just realised her mother was still a very attractive woman, and that 'Uncle Jim' had been a frequent visitor since Daddy died. That Mummy always asked for his advice before she did anything important. She'd been too wrapped up in her own affairs to realise that her broken engagement to Dick might have put things back for her mother too. Maybe it was time she did take some living-in jobs, and give her mother more time to herself. She'd been a selfish little brute, expecting to be waited on, have her meals cooked, her laundry done. For a long time though Asta admitted to herself, she'd thought of the possibility of her mother's marrying again, making her somewhat cool to Jim's friendly advances.

Buttoning her gaberdine coat as she went, Asta had nearly reached the front door when her mother ran after her, flourishing a small leather case. "You won't get far without this, dear," she said. "No need to rush, I've just remembered that kitchen clock is ten minutes fast. I wonder whether Larry could fix that?"

"I wouldn't be at all surprised," said Asta, dryly. "And do stop looking for possible husbands for me, even if electricians *are* scarce. I'm still only twenty-two, you know. You needn't start worrying about me yet. I'm perfectly happy as I am."

Mrs Milne's look was dubious. "You can't fool me, dear. You haven't looked yourself since breaking it off with Dick, you know. After all, it wouldn't hurt to just be friendly with Larry. I think he's lonely too."

"I'm *not* lonely," answered Asta, a trifle too emphatically. "You know I'm against making close friends of neighbours. I shouldn't even be able to run round to the post-box without bumping into him."

Then, in a flippant voice, "I hear they're running home maintenance classes at the local tec. It might be a good idea if I went to them. Or better still, if you did. Then we'd be independent of all these do-it-yourself boffins."

Closing the front door behind her, Asta could see that the young man from next door was standing so close to her own front gate it would be impossible to ignore him. Anyway, he gave a broad smile and introduced himself. "I'm Larry," he said, "Larry Groves. "I lodge next door, with Mrs Biggs. I'm trying to convince our friend here that you won't get your car through that small space."

"Oh!" she said, indignantly, "And I suppose *you* could?"

The smile froze on his face, to be replaced by a look of slight annoyance. "No reflection on your driving, I assure you. However excellent it may be, it'll be a tight squeeze."

Ignoring him, and with small white teeth set in annoyance, Asta unlocked her garage doors, started the Mini's engine, and taking absolutely no notice of his 'left lock, now straighten up a bit' scraped a generous portion of dark blue paint from the Mini's front wing.

Seething inside, but with a set expression, she got out of the car to inspect the damage. He had already crossed the path and was running a long brown forefinger over the mark.

"Hardly worth claiming on the insurance," he said, "you don't want to lose your no-claims bonus. That is — "

"If I still have one, I presume you were going to say, Mr Groves. If it hadn't been for your standing there 'helping' I'd have got out perfectly well, as I always do."

"Sorry," he answered tersely, and turned away. Then over his shoulder, "I'll spray that for you, if you'll get some matching paint. Especially as it seems to have been my fault." He turned away, whistling, but it sounded slightly forlorn.

"Please don't bother," she said, stiffly. Then turning to the American, who was still sitting at the wheel of his car, obviously waiting for her to drive off and make room for him, "If I can't get into my garage when I come home tonight, I shall ring up the police and complain. It's an offence to block the entrance to someone else's drive."

Nose in the air, Asta drove off,

after making the noisiest gear change since she'd taken her driving test. No doubt they were both there watching, she thought. Men!

If she hadn't made it obvious now that she didn't want to know the man next door, he must be pretty thick-skinned, that's all. Asta wasn't quite sure why she'd taken such a dislike to him. He was more than passable to look at, even in his working clothes. He must have a way with older women, judging by the way both Mummy and Mrs Biggs were singing his praises. Nothing wrong with his manners, either, even if he was a little too self-assured. With women, anyway. Pity he couldn't be a little more forthright with that wretched American. She'd often thought how important voices were. His was a deep bass, with a hint of the wide open spaces he'd come from.

She gave herself a little shake. A voice isn't everything. Wheedling his way into her home like that was intolerable. Give the man any encouragement and he'd be always there, no doubt, whistling out of tune and cluttering up the place with his screwdrivers and hammers.

Standing at the lights for a few moments, Asta's eyes were caught by the slightly lighter band of skin on the third finger of her left hand. Until last week she'd been wearing a single stone diamond ring, something that had made all her friends gasp and wonder whether it was real, or one of those clever imitations they were selling now.

Her engagement to Dick had been too recent not to hurt still, and not just a little sometimes, when you were alone in your room, and hadn't to put on a brave face. Sleeping badly was beginning to make her a little nervous too. That scene just now, for instance. Being so rude to someone who was only trying to be helpful, after all. No need to have been quite so bitchy.

It was no use pretending that breaking off an engagement when you hadn't quarrelled, when nothing had really changed, wasn't difficult to cope with. It made you feel so guilty, for one thing. Throwing over a nice boy like Dick, who loved you, and had been stunned at your change of heart.

She hadn't even been able to say 'I don't love you any more' with any conviction, either, because she didn't really know. Maybe it *was* just a case of pre-wedding blues, as Brenda had suggested. Possibly it was just the thought of giving up her independence, of settling down in that bungalow they'd been on the verge of signing the papers for.

"All right, Asta Milne," she muttered, as she dodged round the back streets to avoid the worst of the London traffic. "It's not the end of the world. You'll get over it. After all, it was entirely your own decision. There's no need to go around acting like an embittered old maid." Only time would tell whether it had been the right thing to do, and whether she'd regret it.

There just wasn't any real explanation, nothing you could tell anyone about. She really had thought she was deeply in love with Dick. There had been a time, not so very long ago, when just to hear his name spoken would set her heart beating wildly. Her real love affair, and she'd expected so much from it. Too much, perhaps, for slowly at first, then with deepening conviction, came the realisation that her charming Dick was, at thirty, very much the same as he might have been at thirteen. Vivacious, generous, loving, intelligent enough, and yet a chance remark from one of her friends, after a few drinks at a party, "Your Dick's a trifle Peter Pannish, isn't he? A most delightful person, of course, darling, with such rare boyishness. One gets the feeling that he'll always stay the same. I wonder if he has a secret recipe?"

Playing Wendy to his Peter might have worked, but it seemed a terrific risk, and her friend's remarks jolted Asta considerably.

Everyone said Dick had a great sense of humour, and he was tremendously popular in their circle, but Asta had wondered once or twice, not without a feeling of disloyalty, that the fact of his always paying for more than his fair share of drinks in a pub mightn't have had something to do with it.

How hurt and bewildered he had been when she gave him back his ring. Yet she wondered if it hadn't been something like watching a small boy whose train set had been confiscated. Perhaps she should have gone on playing?

All their friends were amazed when they heard of the broken engagement. Some of them made it pretty plain to Asta that they thought poor old Dick had been treated badly. Even Brenda, her cousin, who'd always been on her side before.

"What's wrong with Dick's boyishness?" she'd asked, her big brown eyes wide with astonishment. "I thought you two were bonkers over each other. Surely it's one of his greatest charms, Asta? Imagine what a stunning father he'd make. He had the kids in stitches at Jane's wedding. Crawling about on the floor with them. He simply adores children."

Asta had considered this. "I know, Bren," she said, at last, "but once they grew out of the 'ring a ring of roses' stage, I wonder whether he'd want to help them with their maths homework? I doubt it."

"You're crazy," was Brenda's answer. "It doesn't pay to look that far ahead. I thought you *loved* Dick. If you go on analysing people like that, you'll end up in my boss's chair, answering all those potty letters people send in to the magazine. Making up all these impossible situations will send you round the bend, old girl. You *can't* analyse a man like Dick, he's unique."

"It's part of my job as a nurse to analyse people, Bren. That old saying about a leopard never changing his spots has a lot to be said for it."

"Well, you can get too critical, too introspective, you know. I can't help feeling that's what's happened to your engagement. You knew what Dick was like when you accepted him. You're the one who's changed, Asta, and if you go on like that you'll never find a man to come up to your standard."

"Maybe it is my fault," came the reply, "maybe marrying Dick might have worked out, but once doubts creep into your mind, it's better not to take a chance."

Although she hadn't been able to explain it to anyone, Asta knew it had all started when she'd met Dick's parents for the first time. His mother, determinedly hospitable with about five kinds of cake, but finding it hard to hide the hostility she felt for the girl who was going to take away her only son. She treated both her husband and son like children, Asta thought, spoiling them, anticipating their every wish, waiting on them.

Dick's father was a heavy advertisement for his wife's cooking, a red-faced man whose welcoming kiss had lingered just a fraction too long on Asta's lips. His gargantuan pepper and salt moustache had made her feel as though she was being embraced by a Yeti. His whole life appeared to revolve round a troop of Boy Scouts.

Fair enough, she decided, a very good thing to do with your spare time, until she realised that the whole of his conversation consisted of nothing but his preparations for taking the troop camping in the summer. It didn't take her many minutes to find out that whatever subject was introduced into the talk, before you knew it, you were back with the Scouts, having reef-knots demonstrated on the piece of cord produced from his pocket. Trying to remember the name of your Guide mistress when you were at school, and which year the new uniforms came in. Before tea was cleared, he had them all tapping out messages in Morse on the tablecloth.

"Where do you go for your own holidays?" she asked the silent mother in a polite effort to bring her into the conversation.

"Holidays?" Her husband's rubicund face, where some small remnants of swiss-roll clung to the moustache, looked perplexed, as he answered the question on her behalf, which seemed a habit of his. "Do you mean by herself? Mother doesn't care for camping, do you, m'dear? Wish I could interest her in the movement, I assure you, Asta. She could be jolly useful helping some of my boys with their cookery badges."

Asta, astonished at such a display of selfishness said, later, in Dick's arms, "Darling, don't you think your mother needs a holiday? She looks so tired."

He looked into Asta's face with a puzzled expression. "Mother? She loves being at home, sweetheart. It's her whole life, I do assure you." He resolved his bewilderment with a few long, tender kisses, then "I can't wait to get you into our own little home, my darling. Waiting there for me every evening. It'll be Heaven! I hate you working as you do. It wouldn't be so bad if all your patients were women, but that last one, wasn't he a racing driver? I can't bear to think of you, touching him."

"Surely, you're not jealous?" she asked, taken aback.

"Of course I am, insanely jealous. I'm old-fashioned enough to believe that a woman's place is in the home, and I'll work like any slave to make sure that ours is a comfortable one, my precious darling. You shall have the best of everything I can get for you."

Suddenly, Dick's handsome young face had turned into a big red one with a huge moustache. It had been so real she'd drawn away from his arms. Strange that she hadn't noticed until now how like his father Dick was. That hearty laughter at his own jokes.

That had always irritated her a little.

That night, Asta had tossed and turned on her bed until early morning. One part of her brain kept telling her not to be stupid, that she still loved Dick madly. How could he possibly be as childish as she was imagining? He had a responsible, well-paid job, hadn't he? Of *course* he wouldn't get like his father, not if you refused to allow him to make a doormat out of you. His mother had spoiled them both, and it's her own fault.

It wasn't any use, though, once she'd started to analyse Dick. There were the things he preferred on TV, for instance, zany American comedies that had him roaring with laughter while she was bored into wide yawns he was too absorbed to notice. Were you going to be able to put up with that, night after night, year after year?

His conversation, too, was a little slick, full of ancient clichés and jargon that had been out for years. The infuriating way some hangers-on took advantage of his free and easy ways. Their 'good old Dick' sounded like an insult some days.

When she'd told her mother of the broken engagement, — there had been surprise, sympathy, but far from perfect understanding.

"Have you thought how humiliated Dick must be feeling, Asta?" she asked. "I wonder if you aren't expecting too much, dear. Marriage must have a lot of give and take, you know. You both have to work on it."

"Yes," Asta replied, wearily, "but you don't have to slave at it, do you? A wedding ring needn't turn into a dog-collar."

2

MRS ADAMS, SRN, ex-Army Medical Service, and part owner of the Rodney Agency moved a long ruler, a plastic container of paper clips, another of rubber bands, and a pencil sharpener in the shape of a tank into the precise positions she liked them to occupy on her impressive desk.

She consulted an attendance register before her with a slight frown, and biro in hand, hesitated over the space where Asta Milne's name appeared. Her slightly pinched nostrils fidgeted. Her long service with the British Army had left her with a phobia about punctuality.

She paid her temporary nurses well, but she expected, and got, conscientious work from them.

"Ah!" she said, darting a look at

Asta's cheeks, pink with the exertion of climbing three flights of stairs. "Nurse Milne. I was just about to mark you absent."

Asta's spirits sagged a little. When Mrs Adams called you by your surname, she wasn't pleased. Then she gave a little flicker of annoyance. She wasn't in the habit of being late, but the traffic had been particularly bad, and Mrs Adams was making her feel like a first year nurse who'd broken some hospital rule.

Steely grey eyes flashed to the clock on the wall, which ticked two or three more seconds on to Asta's debit side before the crisp voice said "Traffic again, I presume?"

She motioned to a chair in front of her desk, and ran a bony finger down the contents of a page she turned to in her register.

"I see you have been with us for over a year now, Nurse. By the terms of your contract you should have done a spell of night duty by now. It's hardly

35

fair to the others if you don't, is it? How do you feel about it?"

Asta grimaced. "I've never been terribly keen on night duty Mrs Adams. As you know, my mother was ill for some time, and I had to get home every day."

"Ah! But your mother is quite recovered now, I take it? I know she's not an old lady who cannot take care of herself."

"No indeed," said Asta, smiling at the thought of her extremely young-looking mother being categorised as an aged parent. "Of course, she likes having me at home, and the work suits me. However, as you say, I have been getting preferential treatment, and I'm quite willing to pull my weight. I did have a letter from the Senior Nursing Office at St Margaret's Hospital, a few weeks ago, asking if I'd be interested in returning there as a staff nurse. Naturally, I have a soft spot for the place, I did my training there, but . . ."

"The pay here is considerably more,"

said Mrs Adams, quickly, "and you have a great deal more freedom, don't you, Asta?"

Noticing the change to her Christian name with some amusement, Asta replied, "Yes, I don't mind admitting that. Mummy had to give up her job when she was ill. My father died two years ago, and we've had an awful lot of expenses. I had been trying to save up for my wedding, too, though I fully intended to go on working after it. I didn't think the work of running a small bungalow would have been enough to keep me occupied. Not until I had a family, anyway."

Mrs Adams's eyes went to Asta's left hand, and noted the absence of the ring. "You speak in the past tense, Asta," she said, a more human note creeping into her voice. "Have you changed your mind about marrying?"

Shrugging her shoulders, Asta said "I'm not sure whether I changed my mind, or my mind changed me, anyway, it's all off now."

"I'm sorry, my dear, very sorry. You looked so radiant on the day you told me. But I'm sure you must have good reason."

Fiddling with the strap of her bag, to gain time, and steady the trembling of her voice, Asta said "Thank you, Mrs Adams, but I'd rather forget all about it. It wasn't an easy decision to make. I could go back to St Margaret's now, I suppose, but I like working this way. However difficult a patient may be you do get right away every evening. You tend to gravitate to the nurses' sitting room if you're in the hospital, and talk shop with the others. All very well for a nurse who hasn't a home near."

Mrs Adams was riffling through a sheaf of papers on her desk. "I wonder how you feel about going back to St Margaret's on a temporary basis, from here, I mean? I have a letter here from the Senior Nursing Officer, who's an old friend of mine. Mrs Danesbury; but of course, you'll know her, won't you? They are simply desperate for nurses. They have thirty or more down with this virus that's been going around. I've already sent them several girls, but they need night staff. Would you consider it, Asta? It may only be for a week or two, depending on what happens. I understand they've got it under control, but a lot of their nurses won't be fit for duty at once, naturally."

Watching Asta's hesitant expression, she coaxed, "It'll be good pay, at staff nurse's rate. We can all use a little extra these days, can't we?"

There was a rueful smile on Asta's lips as she replied "I agree, Mrs Adams. There's the tax and insurance on my car coming up soon, and my mother says the sitting-room curtains are a disgrace. Yes, I'll do it. I'd rather it had been day duty, naturally, but at least it won't be in a strange hospital where I won't know my way about."

She laughed, "It's to be hoped that the skeleton in the lecture room doesn't still rattle along the corridors at night.

I'll never forget my first night on duty. Some of the nurses dressed him up and left him propped up against the vending machine where they knew I'd be sure to go for a coffee. In the half light, I took him for a patient who'd lost his way, and took him by the arm. I yelled so loudly it woke up half the patients, and there was pandemonium. They locked him up after that, but I've never forgotten the horrible *boniness* of that arm."

"Well," said Mrs Adams, with unaccustomed jollity, "I've yet to meet a well-nourished skeleton. It was a silly trick to play, though. I hope it hasn't made you nervous."

"Not really," said Asta. "When would you like me to start duty?"

"Could you manage tonight, Asta? I know its terribly short notice, but they really are in a jam at St Margaret's. Mrs Danesbury says they've already had to close several wards for lack of staff."

"Oh dear," said Asta, "that *is*

sudden. Still, I suppose I could make it. I'd have to go home, of course. I'll need to pack my things. I presume I'll be expected to live in while the emergency lasts?"

"Of course, my dear girl. If you go home straight away, you'll be able to get several hours sleep, won't you? They won't expect you until eight o'clock, but it would be better to report in a little before that, so that they can show you your room and so on."

Not much chance she would be able to sleep, Asta thought. It was rather exciting to be going back to St Margaret's after all. This would be a chance to see whether she would like to go back there permanently.

There had been a lot of changes at the hospital in the past few years. The new Nurses' Block was finished now, and she'd heard reports from Vivian Walker, whom she met occasionally for lunch. Vivian had trained with her, and was now a Staff Nurse.

"I never want to be a Sister," Vivian had told her, her slightly protuberant blue eyes and long features under a straight page-cut serious. "It's far too much responsibility. I'm quite happy to be second in command, and have someone else to refer to. Now you, Asta, you're so cool-headed, so sure of yourself."

The phrase came back to Asta's mind now. "So sure of yourself." It sounded different now, and not the compliment Vivian had meant it to be. She had been so sure of her love for Dick, so positive that it had been the real thing. Well, it would make her more careful in the future. It was going to take a lot more than the attraction of the male and female to make her want to marry anyone else. A great deal more than a lot of what the American's called 'sweet-talk' to ever convince her again.

Asta rose, and picked up her bag. "I'll be going then, Mrs Adams," she said, "I'll have a lot to do when I get home. I don't suppose Mummy will be too pleased at the news. Still, she knew it would come some time, I was only telling her so last week."

Mrs Adams gave one of her rare smiles. "Thank you, Asta," she said, gratefully, "I knew I could count on you. Mrs Danesbury says they've allocated you one of the best rooms, overlooking the gardens. It even has its own shower. Rather different from when I was in the Army, I can tell you. It will certainly be less tiring to live in at the hospital, won't it? Night Duty combined with travelling through the London traffic would be very exhausting."

Nodding her head in agreement, Asta said, "Yes, you're right. Now that my mother is quite well again, I'm sure she won't mind being left, she has plenty of friends and interests."

Scribbling something on a small pink card, Mrs Adams handed it to Asta. "Just give this to Mrs Danesbury when you arrive, will you? I hope she won't persuade you to go back to St Margaret's permanently. You're doing a good job here, Asta. People do like to be nursed in their own homes, and we so often can relieve the problem in a situation like this one. Can you manage four nights a week? It might be five just while this emergency lasts."

As Asta returned to the car park, and noticed the scratch on the side of her Mini once more, she wrinkled her nose at the recollection of that morning's incident. As she put her key into the car door, a thought struck her. Hadn't her mother said that Larry fellow was doing a refresher course at St Margaret's? It was to be hoped their paths wouldn't cross too often. Not that it was likely, with her on night duty, and the hospital being such a vast place.

She had absolutely no intention of getting involved with him, or anyone else, for that matter.

Now that her mother was fully

recovered, and had Jim round there practically every evening, perhaps she could think again about that old dream of going abroad, getting a job in Canada, or Australia, perhaps, and seeing the world. Somewhere nice — or even somewhere nasty, come to that. There was her old friend Betty Carstairs out in Kenya. She'd written quite recently, saying what a crying need there was for trained nurses out there. That would be *real* nursing.

Parting from Dick was still causing her a few tears in the privacy of her bedroom. Maybe the best thing would be to cut herself right off and not be tempted to even consider whether she'd been too hasty.

There were still times when she remembered how kind and sweet Dick had always been to her. No sense in pretending she didn't miss him. Her mother was right, marriage was what you made of it, and the way ahead looked bleak and lonely.

With the rush hour over, the streets

were comparatively easy to negotiate on the way back to Coulsdon. It started to rain, just a few drops at first, then a steady lashing downpour the windscreen wipers could barely cope with. She wasn't sure there hadn't been a distant clap of thunder. The one thing Asta really hated was a thunderstorm. No use telling herself that by the time you heard the thunder the danger was over. She raced the last mile home, determined to reach the safety of her own house before the storm got any worse.

The man next door was just coming out of his gate, and she saw him dive back into the hallway, as if to avoid seeing her.

Asta's eyebrows raised a little, then she shrugged. So he had taken offence at her attitude this morning. Well, perhaps she had been a bit rude. Never mind, she hadn't wanted to encourage him, after all. Getting out of the car, she was startled to hear a deep voice at her elbow, "Here. I borrowed a brolly from Mrs Biggs's hall-stand. Take it and run, it's belting down. I'll shut the garage for you."

A firm hand on Asta's back started her on her way, and she gave in. There wasn't much sense in arguing in the rain.

Then to her horror, a sheet of lightning bounced off the glistening rooftops quite near at hand, followed by a tremendous clap of thunder over their heads. Asta, so cool-headed in most situations, was taken off guard. With a little cry of dismay, she clutched on to Larry's arm, trembling all over.

In one of those blind, primitive fears she rushed for the nearest cover, burying her face in his jacket. Knocking the umbrella from her shaking hands, he pulled her back into the garage. Both arms around her, he patted her back in an avuncular way.

"Nothing to worry about," he comforted, "It'll all be over soon."

Striving hard to regain control and a little dignity, she pulled herself away, but a further flash sent her back to the shelter of his arms, and made her hide her ears with both hands. The scent of his damp Harris-tweed jacket reminded her of the Scottish moors, a good masculine smell.

Cautiously, she raised her head, to meet his quizzical grey eyes. Of course the brute was laughing at her. She seemed fated to make a fool of herself when he was around.

"I apologise for making such an exhibition of myself," she said, stiffly.

There was a twinkle in his eye as he gave a slight bow and said "Any time, dear lady. Rescuing damsels in distress gives me the greatest pleasure, I do assure you. I think the worst of the storm has passed, it must be somewhere over Croydon by now. Hang on to my arm," he said, rescuing the umbrella, "we'll make it to your front door before there are any more drum-rolls. There's your mother looking out of the window."

The front door opened as they

arrived at the small brick porch, and Asta's mother opened the door, with a worried expression on her face. "What on earth are you doing at home, dear? Is something wrong? You're not ill? I heard the garage doors open and the car drive in. I imagined you'd be safely inside somewhere, Asta. I know how you hate storms."

Without waiting for answers to her questions she ushered them into the living room, where a bright fire was burning in the grate. "Why, you're both soaked," she said. "I'll get some towels, and you'd better take off those wet coats."

"I came home because I'm going on night duty," said Asta, kneeling down before the flames, and rubbing her wet hair with the towel. "I'm supposed to get some sleep now, then report to St Margaret's before eight o'clock. I know it's very sudden, but they're evidently very short of nurses. An epidemic of some virus disease Mrs Adams says. I couldn't very well refuse, she's been so good at giving me jobs where I could get home every evening."

"She might have given you a little more time," said her mother, indignantly. "Eight o'clock this evening? You'll only get three or four hours sleep at most. It's too bad. Did you say St Margaret's, where you did your training? Does that mean you're going back there for good? You haven't said anything about it, dear. It's such a quick decision, and on nights, too. I used to hate nights when I was nursing, but at least we had a full day off before we changed over from day duty. How can they expect you to keep awake all night tonight?"

"I'm not going back for good," explained Asta, "this is purely an emergency, and I shall be paid by the agency in the usual way. I expect I shall enjoy being there once I've settled in and got used to sleeping by day. You have to make the switch sometime. I don't suppose that if I had several days to prepare for it

I'd get much sleep in the day. I shall be lodging at the hospital while the job lasts, Mummy. My bedroom faces the road here, doesn't it? They have a special block for night-duty staff at the hospital, away from the noise."

"I still think it's too sudden," said her mother, crossly, cutting one of her special chocolate sponges into wedges. "It's too early to cook you a proper lunch. I'll call you at six, and you can have a meal then. Perhaps *you* would like to — ?" She looked round, but Larry had disappeared into the hall, and they heard the front door open. "Surely he hasn't gone without a word?" she said. "Have you been rude to him again, Asta, it's really too bad, you know."

Asta was about to make an indignant reply when Larry came bounding in again, carrying what appeared to be a child's furry toy.

"What ever have you got there?" asked Mrs Milne.

"It doesn't appear very salubrious, I must say."

Larry came over to the fire, and exhibited his find. They could see it was a tiny kitten, bedraggled and faintly mewing in one of his big hands. "I thought I saw something move under the bushes," he said, "just as we came in. Thought I'd investigate. Poor little chap, he's wet through."

Asta handed him a towel, and he tenderly dried the tiny animal's black and white fur. "He's rather nice, isn't he? I wonder how he came to be under those bushes. A pretty hard-hearted owner to turn him out in this weather."

"He doesn't belong to any of the immediate neighbours," said Mrs Milne pouring milk into a saucer and putting it down in front of the hearth. "Why the poor little thing's starving. It's almost too weak to lap."

After a few minutes, the little cat's fur began to dry into a fluffy ball, and it's amber eyes surveying the room, it decided to curl up on the wool hearthrug and fall fast asleep.

"What are we going to do with you, old chap?" asked Larry, with a worried look. "Unless we find where you come from, it looks like the RSPCA for you. I'd have you myself but I know from the way she chases cats from the garden Mrs Biggs isn't a likely owner for you."

There was something about the way he handled the little creature, the trouble in his voice, that made Asta say, quickly, "We could do with a cat, couldn't we, Mummy? You were only saying last week that you thought you'd seen a mouse in the kitchen. Do say we can keep him. That is, unless we discover the owner, though I don't think they deserve to keep a pet, turning such a tiny kitten out in a storm."

Mrs Milne stroked the kitten with one finger, and they were all delighted to hear the faintest little purr. "Of course we can, Larry."

"I'll buy it a crate of cat food,"

he said delightedly. "I'm a dog man myself, I've two red setters in Australia, but I'm a sucker for any animal."

For some stupid reason, Asta's mind had to go back to Dick. He had quite a job hiding his positive dislike of both cats and dogs. Strange in a man who appeared to love small children so much. Or could that have been just another bid for popularity — another of the 'good old Dick' things? She'd thought, once, when they were engaged to be married, what a pity it would be if their children were to be deprived of the joys of keeping a pet. She'd always had one as a child, and remembered the fun it had been.

It was to be hoped the man next door wouldn't make that kitten an excuse for eternally popping in and out to see how it was. Still, it wasn't going to matter so much now; she'd be away at St Margaret's, after all.

She hadn't filled in the diary she'd kept since schooldays in the past few days, so sat down at the dressing-table in her blue silk dressing-gown, pen in hand.

'I must admit,' she wrote, 'that man who lodges with Mrs Biggs can grow on you. Not that I have any intention of allowing him get too big in *my* life. I hope I've learnt a lesson. Naturally I'm missing the good times Dick and I had together, I'm bound to. Better to have a few regrets now, though, than wait until after we were married.

"It was funny to see a great husky man like Larry so concerned over a kitten. It looked such a scrap in his huge hands. I did make a fool of myself over that storm, acting like a great kid. I'm furious with myself, after this morning, when I snubbed him so badly. Perhaps it will be a good thing to go back to St Margaret's for a spell. Fun to meet some of the nurses I knew. Satisfaction in helping out in a crisis.

'Dick's photograph is still on my dressing table, I keep meaning to get rid of it. It seems a bit like rubbing salt into the wounds to just send it back to him. I know he had it specially taken for me, and bought that antique silver frame for it, too.' Putting the diary back in its drawer, and picking up the photo, Asta studied Dick's features. They were still the same as when she'd been so much in love with him, weren't they? He was handsome, virile, intelligent. What *was* wrong with her? What was she looking for? All that stuff about wanting her in the home, wasn't that natural? Most women would be pleased.

Resolutely, she placed the frame in her drawer. Perhaps later, when Dick had time to get over it, she'd send it back. After all, the frame must have cost him an awful lot. A trifle pretentious, perhaps, but wasn't that better than being mean?

If only you could understand your own feelings, she sighed, let alone someone else's.

Last night she hadn't slept well, and now, with the blinds down, and snuggled blissfully under her warm duvet, with the sound of rain, more gentle now, on the windowpanes, acting as a lullaby, Asta did some of the relaxing exercises she'd learned some time before, letting her whole body go limp, spreading her hands, palm down, on the sheet, unclenching the tautness of her jaw.

Gradually, the water-colour of a scene in the Highlands, which she'd picked up in a junk shop, the gilt oval mirror hanging on the wall, the rosy-pink curtains that matched her duvet, and the bookcase of brightly-coloured paperbacks, all merged into a dim kaleidoscope of hues and she slept.

It was dusk when her mother came into the room, with a cup of tea in one hand which she placed on the little bedside table.

"I'm waking you in plenty of time," she said, "I didn't want you to go on duty at St Margaret's without a good meal inside you. I've been all along the road, but no one seems to have lost a kitten. It's a dear little thing,

I shall be glad to give it a home. It seems quite recovered, and is prowling all over the kitchen. Larry suggests we call him 'Blitz'."

Asta yawned sleepily. "I've had such a marvellous sleep. It won't be at all difficult to keep awake tonight now. Do you know, Mummy, I'm quite looking forward to going back to St Margaret's. I hope there will still be lots of nurses I know there. Life's been a bit hum-drum lately, it'll do me good to be among people again."

"I'm going to miss you, dear," said her mother, "it's been lovely having you home for the past year or so."

"Oh!" said Asta, "you haven't lost me, I shall be popping too and fro whenever I'm free. This job isn't for good, you know, just as long as the emergency lasts."

Her mother hesitated. "Dick called. He brought a lovely bunch of red roses, which he said were for me, but he looked very disappointed when I told him I couldn't disturb you.

He's still in love with you, Asta. No, he didn't say anything, but the poor boy looks so woebegone. I still think you've been hard on him, dear. Not that I'm advocating marrying someone you don't love — not for a moment, darling, you know your own feelings best, naturally. I still can't understand how you could have let things go so far as nearly buying a house before you decided not to marry him after all. I suppose — there isn't anyone else, is there? That would explain a lot, of course, though you've never mentioned anyone."

"No, of course there's no one else," said Asta. "I just want to be free, that's all. I'd rather you didn't tell Dick where I've gone, I don't want him following me to St Margaret's. I expect I'm being a bit silly, expecting too much. One of these days I may look back and think I made a bad mistake in refusing a man like Dick, who could give me a nice home, children, maybe, all the things most girls are looking for.

But I can't help the conviction, deep down inside, Mummy, that there is something more, something that will sweep me off my feet, and marry a man, no matter what he looks like, or does."

"You may be right, my dear," said her mother, "I do hope you will meet the right man some day, just as I did."

3

LARRY GROVES'S landlady, vast-bosomed, blue-aproned and loquacious, endeavoured to mother all her boarders as only a frustrated woman with a highly developed maternal instinct can. What she lacked in cooking ability was made up for in kindness.

Mrs Biggs always knew where to lay her hand on anything, except for rather frequently lost 'h's' a mortifying reminder of her East End roots, before an obliging stage manager had placed her in the front row of the chorus purely on the strength of her legs.

There were numerous reminders of those happy days in photos of herself when young, in varying amounts of sequins and feathers, all scattered around the house on every space that presented itself.

These artistic efforts merely underlined the fact that Mrs Biggs's normal footwear, wide and comfortable slippers for the most part, had replaced the dainty silver shoes she had once worn. Those legs, now painfully mapped out with blue veins had once been elegant enough to tempt the late Captain Biggs into Holy Matrimony, a state he'd successfully avoided for the first fifty years of his life.

Being pitched into such respectability had made Mrs Biggs very mindful of her neighbour's morality.

Carefully placing Larry's breakfast bacon and eggs in front of him on the breakfast table, she lingered to brush an imaginary speck from the tablecloth.

Larry gave a little sigh of surrender. When Mrs Biggs lingered, it was a sign she wanted a little chat. After a series of much worse landladies, Larry felt that sparing a few minutes to listen sometimes was a small price to pay for really clean lodgings and passable food.

Indicating the bright sunshine with one vast hand, as though she had just waved a wand for it she said "Lovely day after the storm, Mr Groves."

"Still looks a bit nasty over there," said Larry, smiling at her, and glancing at a large black cloud over the grey slates of the rooftops opposite.

His landlady's bright, sandy-lashed eyes went to a silver framed portrait on the mantelpiece, flanked by two portraits of herself as principal boy in *Puss in Boots*. It was a photo of her late husband, Albert, of the Mercantile Marine. Dead many years before, but still consulted in times of trouble as he had been in life.

"You're right, Mr Groves. My Albert always 'ad 'is doubts this kind of morning. Too good to last, 'e'd say."

This time it was obvious Mrs Biggs really *had* something to say. Recognising her need to communicate, Larry regretfully put an old envelope to keep his place in the book he was studying, held out his cup for more

63

coffee from the pot she was holding, and resigned himself.

Smiling good-naturedly, he said "the barometer's going back again, I'm afraid."

"Ah! My Albert thought the world of that barometer. Always tapped it first thing when 'e was at 'ome. Much better at telling the weather than all them TV men put together, my Albert was. Comes of being at sea so long, I dare say."

From where she was standing by the side of a gleaming mahogany sideboard, Mrs Biggs could see through her snowy net curtains to the road outside, and frequently took advantage of the fact. Mrs Biggs seldom went out, but she took in a lot from her vantage point. Her equivalent of Captain Biggs's crow's nest, in fact.

"There goes Asta, from next door," she said. "Trained at St Margaret's Hospital, she did. I went there for my varicose veins. My Albert used to say there isn't another hospital as good in the south of England, and 'e should know, seeing 'e died there, poor dear. If they couldn't save 'im no one could, I reckon. A nice girl, Asta, but a bit standoffish. Not that she isn't kind, remembering 'ow good she was to me when I fell in the garden and broke me wrist."

"Oh?" Larry's eyes went back longingly to his book.

"Wouldn't you like some more toast, Mr Groves? No trouble you know. That first lot was a bit burnt. I left it under the grill to go to the door for the post. Mr Tomkins, in the back first-floor room, eats stacks of toast. You should 'ave seen 'im this morning, before you came down, running off for 'is train with a piece still in 'is 'and. Bless 'is heart. I'm very lucky with my boarders this year, I must say. I'd rather deal with men than girls, any time."

She took another look through the window. "Especially modern girls, Mr Groves. When I was young, the best career for a pretty girl was on the stage, but as soon as I got the chance of a good respectable marriage, I took it, and no regrets. I'd look silly now, dancing round the stage in these, wouldn't I?"

She held up one check patterned slipper with a fluffy pom-pom on the toe.

"Now you take Asta Milne, for instance. Would you credit it, Mr Groves, only the other day the silly girl broke off her engagement to Mr Wilson, one of the nicest, sweetest boys you could wish to know. Boarded with me when 'e was at College, 'e did, before 'is parents moved down from the north. That's 'ow they met. Over the garden wall, as you might say. Such nice manners, Mr Wilson 'ad. Always stopped and 'ad a word with me when 'e called on Asta. If I 'appened to be looking out, that is. Always up to some trick or other, 'e was, made you roll up. Just like a big schoolboy."

Mrs Biggs's plump fingers went through the motion of clicking. "Then,

66

just like that, she broke off the engagement, Mr Groves. There wasn't anyone else, either, not that I 'eard of, she just changed 'er mind, that's all. Broken-'earted 'e was, you could tell. Like a kid what doesn't know what it's being smacked for. Mr Tomkins is a friend of the Wilson family. Says poor Mr Wilson was flabbergasted. Asta didn't tell 'im why she wouldn't marry 'im, didn't even make any proper excuse, seemingly, just gave 'im back 'is ring. A real beauty that was, too, must 'ave cost a packet."

"Perhaps she decided her career was more important to her," shrugged Larry, buttering another piece of toast. Discussing other people's shattered romances was hardly his metier, he decided. "They say it's a woman's prerogative, don't they? Though some women certainly take advantage of the fact."

Mrs Biggs gave a prolonged sniff. "She must 'ave changed it pretty quick, that's all I can say. Only the day before Mrs Milne told me, about the broken engagement, I mean, I watched Asta and her fiance leave the 'ouse, 'appening to be cleaning the front winders at the time, as I was, and they was looking into each other's eyes like a couple of love-birds. I ask you, Mr Groves, what could make a girl draw back so sudden as that?"

She folded her arms as near as she was able over the blue cotton overall. "Fickle, I calls it. It's an old-fashioned word, I know, but fickle's the only word for such be'aviour. 'Owever nice a girl may be, I don't 'old with that kind of thing. Breaking a poor boy's 'eart just on a whim."

She peered at Larry's plate. "No more toast? I know what my Albert would 'ave said, 'your word should be your bond' was 'is motto."

Picking up the portrait of her extremely hirsute husband, she breathed on the glass and gave it a quick rub with the corner of her overall.

"I thought I'd tell you, Mr Groves,

seeing as you're friendly with Asta's Mum, and in and out of the 'ouse, like. She's an attractive girl, and I wouldn't like to see anyone else get hurt. Her mother's very grateful for all the little jobs you've done for 'er, she often says so."

"Thank you, Mrs Biggs," said Larry, with the suspicion of a smile at the corners of his generous mouth. "There's no danger of my being caught I do assure you. I'm much too busy with my work to get involved with a love affair. Not that Miss Milne has shown any signs of interest in me — rather the reverse, in fact."

Mrs Biggs's voice sank to a confidential whisper, after a hasty glance over her shoulder as though she suspected being overheard. "Mrs Milne 'as a very nice gentleman of 'er own, and I know she wouldn't mind me telling you, but 'e's not so 'andy with his 'ands as you are, Mr Groves. Like my Albert. Put 'im on a ship and 'e could mend anything, but ask 'im to do a little job in the 'ouse, and 'e was flummoxed. In my opinion, Mrs Milne would 'ave married again long ago, if it wasn't for Asta. Now, I suppose she'll 'ave to put it off again, with Asta not getting married after all."

"Pity," said Larry, "sounds as if our Asta is a wee bit selfish."

Mrs Biggs nodded. "I'd like to give that young lady a bit of my mind, and would if she belonged to me."

Picking up his book, Larry said "I shan't be home until late this evening, Mrs Biggs. I'm on call at the hospital, with the shortage of staff. I may even sleep there if it's a busy night."

He looked back at the door. "I've started on my thesis. I hope the clattering of my typewriter doesn't disturb you too much."

"Lord bless you, no, Mr Groves. There's only me and Mr Tomkins now. I can't manage with more than two boarders with my feet playing me up. He's at London University and away all day. No one will 'ear you up there."

"On the days I'm at home," he told her, "if I don't come down to lunch, just leave me, eh, Mrs Biggs? Sometimes I get so engrossed I don't want to leave off."

"Well," said Mrs Biggs, dubiously, "if that's what you wants, Mr Groves. I 'ad another writing gent 'ere once. Used to stay up in his room for days at a time, 'e did. I sometimes listened at the door of 'is room to make sure 'e was still alive." She brightened up, and said "anyways, I can put you an electric kettle up there, and if you don't come down, I'll put a pint of milk outside the door, so you can make coffee. That's what Mr Wannacot used to do. Kept a tin of biscuits up there, 'e did, too. You'd never believe 'ow quick 'e got through a pound of Digestives."

"Suits me fine, Mrs Biggs," said Larry. "I'll keep to that arrangement. Wannacot? The name sounds familiar, somehow."

"Crime novels 'e wrote. 'Ave you read any of them? I 'ave. Leastways,

I've got nearly all of them, autographed, too. Give you the 'orrors, they do, especially that one *Skullcap*. Wrote that up there in your very room, 'e did. Mr Wannacot's got a nice flat in Town now, and runs a Rolls-Royce car. What sort of book are you writing, Mr Groves?"

Larry's face was amused. "Obviously the wrong kind, considering the old banger *I* run. My book is a study of disease among the North American Indians. I'm afraid it'll never be made into paperback."

"That's a pity, after all your work," she said, warmly. "Well, it takes all sort of books to fill the library shelves, I dare say. I likes a good romance myself. Not too short, but not too long-winded. I likes reading what people say to each other."

"Surely," said Larry, with a twinkle in his eyes, "you must have some descriptive passages in a book? It can't be all conversation?"

"It can be, as far as I'm concerned,"

said Mrs Biggs, firmly. "I just skips over the rest. After I've read the last page, to make sure it's going to end happily. You can get through a book a day that way."

Wending his way through the traffic to St Margaret's hospital, Mrs Biggs's story about the girl next door and her broken engagement kept going through his mind. Pictures of his younger brother, Alan kept emerging.

Young Alan whose brain had been so much more brilliant than his own, had shown such great promise. A tall, sunburnt giant of a lad without a care in the world until he'd met Enid, in Sydney.

Alan, with his lithe, athletic body and eyes the colour of a Mediterranean sea. Alan, who'd fallen wildly in love with a more than worldly girl, some years older than himself.

They'd gone everywhere together, surfing, swimming, seeming to have been made for each other. Against their better judgement, both his parents and Larry had taken it for granted that the expensive diamond ring Alan had begged, borrowed and worked for was a commitment to marry. They even got to liking the girl for all the joy she brought to Alan.

Then, all at once, there was a stony remoteness about which he refused to talk. Enid had passed on to another love, taking the ring with her, leaving Alan feeling as empty and useless as one of those plastic beakers cast up on the sands from a passing liner.

After a few weeks, he'd joined a wild mob of motor cyclists, who went roaring up and down the roads out of Sydney with a seeming death wish under their gaily painted helmets.

Alan had died in a multiple crash, and Larry felt sure he'd meant it to happen.

Larry's mouth, which was the wrong shape for bitterness, tightened. He had been very close to his brother.

So here, living next door, was just such another girl as Enid. Making some guy love her, then turning him down for no reason. Leading a man on until he was crazy about her, then having fun watching his heart break.

"I suppose it inflates their egos to have a man feel like that about them!" he muttered through clenched teeth. "As soon as they're sure of victory, they start looking round for someone else. Well, it's never going to happen to me."

He recalled that little scene outside the house. There certainly hadn't been any provocative looks from Asta, but maybe her technique was playing hard to get? She didn't quite look the part, but then, neither had Enid, at first. Pity. Mrs Milne was such a nice woman, he really enjoyed going in there to do little things for her. It was pretty plain that money wasn't too free in the Milne household. Some of the rooms hadn't been decorated for years, and there was still a number of things he'd noticed that wanted doing.

"No," he said, angrily clenching his

teeth on an empty pipe, "I just won't be cut off by that snooty little madam. She needn't think I shall offer to spray her car again. If she'd taken the bother to listen to me in the first place she'd never have scratched it. Obstinate little cuss!"

Now she was without a man about the place, he supposed, she'd start looking around. No doubt there would be plenty of blokes who'd find those bright blue eyes and trim figure attractive. If he stayed with Mrs Biggs long enough he'd be watching a procession of eager young men bearing gifts go past his window to call on Asta. Damn women anyway.

He gave an apologetic grin to a policeman who'd been waving him on for some seconds.

And now, back to work. Once his thesis was finished, he'd start thinking of the future. Back to Australia, probably.

Asta would have done her first night on duty by the time he got to the hospital, was probably eating her breakfast in the canteen. First night on must have been a bit rough. She'd probably go straight to bed afterwards. He pulled a face, surprised at his own thoughts. What the Devil did it matter what she was doing?

Just the same, it was pleasant to think of that neat little waist encircled by a dark belt with a silver buckle, she was the type of woman who'd look marvellous in a nurse's uniform. She'd be efficient, too, he was willing to bet.

A much better nurse than she was a driver, he chuckled, remembering that noisy gear change. It must have made her furious.

After he'd parked the car, Larry thought he had a glimpse of Asta, strolling in the grounds, deep in conversation with a couple of other nurses, no mistaking the colour of her hair with the sun shining on it, even from the back. She had a way of walking, with her shoulders pulled straight, a way of listening to someone with her head slightly on one side. Anyway, she appeared to be popular, from the way the others were all laughing. Old colleagues, he supposed, remembering that Asta had trained here at St Margaret's.

It hadn't been too hectic a day at the hospital, after all, a couple of the doctors had recovered enough to be back on duty, so Larry decided to go back to his lodgings.

He'd just finished putting a new washer on Mrs Milne's leaky bathroom tap that evening, and was enjoying a cup of coffee with her when she said "I wonder if you'd like to join our drama group, Larry? We're only amateurs, of course, but we raise quite a lot of money for charity, and it's great fun."

"But I can't act," he said, highly amused at the idea. "You'd be asking for instant disaster if you put me on the stage, Mrs Milne."

"There are lots of things to do

beside the acting," she said, "there's scenery painting, prompting, designing costumes, preparing and printing the programmes, no end of jobs, and never enough people to do them. You're so good with your hands, I know we'd find you invaluable, Larry. I do a lot of the sewing of costumes on my machine, and take part too, sometimes."

"I mostly work in the evenings," he said, "I'm afraid — "

"I've noticed you don't go out much," said Mrs Milne, with a little frown. "It would do you good to meet people. We're doing *White Horse Inn* in a few weeks. We've another Australian boy playing the lead. A dark boy with a lovely voice. Ken. Ken. I can't remember his other name, but I think he comes from Sydney too."

"Not Ken Markham?" asked Larry, eagerly.

"Yes, that's it, do you know him? Well, what a coincidence!"

"We were at College together. I'd very much like to see him again. We seem to have lost touch. I can't promise I'll be of very much use to you in the drama line, but I'll be quite willing to be odd job man."

That evening, after driving Mrs Milne to the school where they rehearsed their plays, she ushered Larry into a small, brightly lit hall, where various pieces of equipment announced that it was the gym, several people whose ages varied from sixteen to the late seventies were milling about. Some, with scripts in their hands were muttering their parts, two of them wrestled with a pair of stage curtains that refused to draw and two little old ladies trotted to and fro with cups and saucers for the half-time break. One lad was emulating a long-distance runner by dashing round the gas heaters that stood along the walls, trying to light as many as possible from what was obviously the last match in the box.

"Here," Larry called to him, "I'm a pipe smoker, take mine. I've another box."

The sandy-haired boy whose snub nose was practically covered by one large freckle, grinned. "New leading man?" he enquired.

"Nothing half as grand," said Larry with a friendly smile. "Just here to lend a hand with the chores, that's all."

He had been introduced to half a dozen or more people by Mrs Milne when there was an explosive shout from the doorway.

"Larry, you old bastard!" Ken's typically Australian greeting fell warmly on Larry's ears. The older members of the Elmchester Drama Group registered varying emotions as Ken rushed across the polished wood floor. Gripping Larry's outstretched hand like a vice, he thumped him heartily on the back.

There was nothing exceptional about Ken Markham. Of average build, he had the barrel chest of a singer. His proudest boast was that he was of Welsh ancestry, his grandparents having emigrated to Australia fifty years before. Straight brown hair fell over his high forehead, impatiently pushed back from his dark brown eyes every few minutes.

"Who was going to write every week, then?" he demanded, giving Larry another slap on the back that would have floored a weakling.

"I haven't noticed the mail man exactly weighted down with letters from you, either," said Larry. "Though I must admit I've moved around a bit since arriving in England. Landlady trouble. OK now, though. It's great to see you, Ken. You're a lot thinner. Been training for the Olympics? As I remember you suffered from that occupational hazard of all singers, a tendency to tubbiness."

Ken looked as if he was going to say something, then, with a shrug, "Must be the British beer, old son. No nourishment in it. Not like the stuff we get at home. There's real body in Toohy's."

It wasn't many minutes before Larry, hammer in hand, was on the top of a tall ladder, fixing parts of the scenery, and disentangling the cords of the reluctant curtains.

"What a find, Mrs Milne, heaven sent." Their producer, Adam Prince, a quaint little man with an absurd French beard and huge flapping ears that might have been a template for Noddy's, minced over. Those ears could pick up the merest whisper from the wings of the stage, and he would bellow in an astonishingly loud voice *"Silence! I will have silence! If you want to gossip, Please go outside!"*

Larry gave him an amused look. "Who's the little Napoleon?" he asked Mrs Milne, in a whisper.

"Just have a guess at what he does for a living," she asked, with a flash of amusement in her eyes.

Larry grimaced. "Artists? Runs a dress shop? Hairdresser? Plays the violin? No? I give up."

She gave a girlish giggle. Larry at once saw how much she was like her daughter. Not that he'd seen Asta smile much since he'd met her.

"He keeps a greengrocer's shop in the High Street. His fruit and vegetables are arranged so artistically you're rather afraid to ask him to spoil the pattern. He's very good at producing our plays, though. You wait, he'll never allow a tall, personable boy like you to go to waste banging in nails. Before you know where you are, he'll have you up on that stage, you'll see."

"Never!" said Larry, firmly. "I'd make a complete ass of myself." They stood looking at the stage, where Ken was getting ready to sing one of his arias. Then, more to make conversation than anything else, Larry said "I wonder your daughter doesn't take part. She has such a nice speaking voice, hasn't she? One couldn't help noticing. It's so much like your own."

"Thank you, Larry," she answered with a pleased look. "Asta did belong to our group before she became engaged to Dick, but he didn't like it. I think he was a little jealous, anyway she gave it up. We miss her very much, I can assure you, I've been hoping she might join us again now . . . but, well, I've not been too happy about Asta just lately, Larry. I haven't wanted to nag her, but she isn't her old fun-loving self any more. I sometimes wonder if she wasn't too hasty, breaking off her engagement like that. They appeared to be so much in love. She simply refuses to discuss why she did it. It's hurt me, we had such a close relationship before."

Larry could see the deep concern on Mrs Milne's face. "Of course," she went on, "I could see that Dick was jealous, he got so very annoyed when Asta stayed rather late one night at an office party, but he was an intelligent man. I'm sure that if Asta had discussed it with him he'd have seen how stupid jealousy is. She misses Dick, I'm sure. She's been at home so much in the evenings, and seems to have dropped all her friends. Of course, they were Dick's friends too, perhaps that's why. Anyway," she said, with a sigh, "Asta will be on night duty for the next few weeks. Maybe seeing some of the nurses she trained with will be good for her. I can't bear to see her so quiet."

"Jealousy can be a very hard thing to live with," said Larry, then stopped. What the devil had it to do with him? A sophisticated girl like Asta could stand up for herself. Then he grinned at the recollection of her slight figure standing on the pavement, telling that American in the big car where he got off. Seems to have worked, too — or perhaps it was his own joking remark. Anyway, the car hadn't been seen since.

At the end of the rehearsal he went with Ken for a drink at the Bear and Tipstaff, nearby. They relaxed over a beer, and swapped tales of what they had been doing since leaving Sydney.

Mrs Milne's friend, Jim Barton, who had a small part in the play, had taken her home. A nice man, Larry thought, quiet, thoughtful, and obviously very fond of her. They still made a handsome pair, she with her beautiful skin and bright eyes, he with a sprinkling of white in his dark curly hair. A pity if Asta was keeping them from making a new start together.

Ken had drained his first pint with hardly a stop for breath, and ordered another before they found a quiet seat in the corner of the crowded bar.

"What are you doing, Ken? Staying in England for long?"

"Got myself a nice little desk in Australia House," came the reply. "Telling the Poms what it's like in God's own country."

Larry raised a quizzical eyebrow. "Why leave it yourself?"

"Music," said Ken, briefly. "I'm getting lessons in the evenings from a tip-top man. He's sure my voice has potential, but it'll need a lot more training, with the stiff competition these days. Joining his drama group is helping me over a hang-up I have about appearing before an audience. That's my main trouble, old chap, something I have to get over, or go under." His voice was bitter. "I did get a wonderful chance one night, in Melbourne, but when it came to the night, I just dried up, couldn't produce a single note."

"Dried up?" Larry's voice was incredulous. "I can't believe it, Ken. You were all right at College, when we produced shows. What happened to you?"

Ken shrugged his massive shoulders and drained his second pint. "Remember Stella?"

Larry made a concentrated mental effort. "Yes, I think so. The little blonde with the deep dimple in her chin?"

"That's Stella. I fell in love with her. Oh! It was the real McCoy, Larry. When I sang — it was to her. I worshipped that girl, and I thought she loved me. Then one evening, when I was singing in a concert, she was standing in the wings with that sarcastic bloke, McWhirter, the Canadian. I'll never forget it. They were poking fun at my singing, you know, miming, and laughing at me. Obviously she didn't know I could see her, but there was a mirror at the side of the stage. It just about slayed me. I didn't think I'd ever sing again."

"Oh come on!" said Larry hotly, "you're not going to let a worthless little bitch like Stella ruin your career, are you, Ken? Can't you take a joke; I don't suppose they meant anything by it at all."

"Every time I went on the stage I could hear her, laughing at me," said Ken morosely. "I thought if I left Australia, I'd be able to forget. So far, though I don't mind doing a bit of singing for an amateur company, I'm still terrified of breaking down in anything important."

"You'll get over it," said Larry, confidently, "of course you will. No girl's worth upsetting your life for. I haven't met the female who'd be even remotely likely to get me off my set course. If I as much as saw one looming on the horizon, I'd pack my bags and be off out of temptation."

"Lucky bastard," said Ken fondly. "But no one's immune, you know. When you do fall, it may be harder than you think." He drained his glass. "Have a short one?"

"No, I won't," said Larry. "I'm driving, but don't let me stop you."

Just about half an hour later, Ken a trifle glassy-eyed, had lost all his inhibitions about singing in public, and raising a glorious tenor voice, brought the rest of the bar to a sudden hush with a rendering of *Rigoletto.* "Wayward is womankind," he sang with feeling, "as feather in the wind."

"True, true," said Larry, "But better be starting for home, hadn't we?"

"Old Verdi knew what he was saying," said Ken, "like feathers, all of 'em."

After he'd left Ken, safely delivered to his flat in Bayswater, with promises of further meetings, Larry drove home through the now deserted streets. The memory of Ken's song kept crowding into his mind.

It was usually the men who were blamed for being unfaithful, but how true was it, after all? Whichever way you turned there were women who seemed to get a kick out of playing with a man's heart. That girl next door, for instance. Why had she gone so far as to let the poor beggar buy an engagement ring, practically buy a house, before she threw him over. Was it his jealousy? Surely he must have shown signs of that before? Some people took it as a sign of love. Maybe she'd given the man cause to be jealous, playing around to test his reactions, then kicking when he really objected.

Yes, that would about fill the bill, he deliberated, pipe clenched between his teeth.

This girl of Ken's, too — Stella. A pretty little piece as he remembered, but had Ken really imagined he was the only one? How blind could love really be? How a man like his friend could have fallen so hard for all that simpering sugarpuff was incredible. There was no accounting for it.

It was a lot easier to choose a mate when girls didn't have careers, he thought, then grinned at his chauvinistic attitude. He could imagine what the independent girl next door would think of that one.

You'd just have to be more careful not to get involved. That fellow Dick had soon found how shallow she was, hadn't he?

He wasn't quite so biased as to imagine that all women were like that, naturally. Mum and Dad had been very happy, after all. There must be plenty of decent girls around. But his young brother's death was still too traumatic. It was going to be years before he'd be able to trust another woman, if ever.

4

VIVIAN WALKER dumped Asta's suitcase on the bright red cover of her duvet. "There!" she puffed. "What do you think of the new nurses' flats? A bit different from the rooms we had when we first started our training together, eh? Running hot water, carpet on the floor, bedside lamp, extra points for all your gadgets, shelves for your books."

"My window looks out on the grounds, too," said Asta. "How lovely all the spring bulbs look. Remember that first room, overlooking the ambulance depot? Only one small rug between our beds, and we used to toss up whose side it should be on for the coming week. I can still feel the chill of that awful vinyl floorcovering, in yucky shades of green and brown. They've certainly gone to town now."

"I'm so glad you're back," said Vivian, eagerly, "St Margaret's has never been the same since you left. Have you had a chance to see the nurses' lounge yet? Or the new library?"

"I did just take a peep into the lounge," said Asta, busily sorting out her clothes and hanging them into a mirror-faced wardrobe. "Colour TV, record player, and enough comfortable armchairs to go round."

Vivian's humorous face broke into a broad grin. "The staff nurses used to hog the armchairs in the old days, didn't they, Asta? I'd been here for over a year before I dared to sit in an armchair, and even then, I leapt out of it when Staff Nurse Weekes came in. And she took it as a right, all she said was 'thanks for keeping it warm, Nurse.'"

Asta's feelings were mixed. She'd really enjoyed her work for the agency, meeting so many people, never having time to get at all bored with a job before you moved on to another. But, of course, she still *was* with the agency, and Mrs Adams might recall her to work somewhere else at any time. She was slipping back so easily into the old atmosphere of St Margaret's it was easy to forget that little fact.

When she'd left there, the new nurses' flats were just a half-finished shell, a muddy mess of bricks, concrete, window-frames and cheerful workmen who whistled at every pretty nurse who passed.

Now, it was finished, and been declared well and truly open by a visiting Royal personage. Not what you could call an architectural masterpiece, but certainly a lot more comfortable to live in.

There were dozens of new faces, of course, many of them black, or Indian.

It was nice to have Vivian chattering on while she finished her unpacking. Even though her thoughts were not entirely with her friend.

"I haven't brought a lot of things with me," she told her. "I shall go home on my first night off, and I can collect anything I want then."

"How long shall you be staying?" asked Vivian, a little wistfully, "when I caught sight of you coming down the drive I thought, Oh! Goody. Here's Asta back. I do hope it will be a long time. We're chronically short of staff even when everybody's well. The past few weeks have been really awful. I had the bug myself, but not very badly. Hope you'll escape it, Asta. They say they have it licked now, so you should be all right."

"I don't know how long it'll be," said Asta, "the agency I work for never keeps a nurse on one job for too long, unless there are special reasons. Afraid of losing them I suppose."

"We shall have to think up that special reason," said Vivian, with a smile. "I wish you'd stop here for good."

"Special reasons," like what? Asta

thought. Getting right away from Dick, for instance. Letting Mummy and Jim get used to being together without her being around too much? No, best not to let other thoughts crowd into your mind, like the hope of running into someone.

Vivian sat on the bed, long legs stretched out straight in front of her, big blue eyes full of questions.

"Asta, stop me if I'm asking too many questions, but last time we had lunch in town together, you were engaged to be married. You were full of plans. You even had the colour of the bedroom curtains decided on. What's happened? You're not wearing that gorgeous diamond ring any more."

She stopped and regarded Asta with a critical air. "Come to mention it, old girl, you don't look your usual blooming self. A bit peaky, I'd say, all eyes. Is it a broken romance, or would you rather not talk about it? Just tell me to shut up and mind my own business and I'll give my famous impersonation of a tongue-tied clam."

Carefully stowing her diary under a pile of undies in the drawer of her dressing table, Asta turned to face Vivian's questions with a calm face.

"I suppose a broken romance is the classic term for it," she said.

"Oh, Asta! Did he treat you badly? The skunk!" Vivian's voice was full of indignation and sympathy. "And you were so much in love."

Asta shrugged. "No, I haven't been jilted, in fact, I was the guilty one. Even now, I wonder at myself, but, well — an engagement isn't quite like any other kind of promise, is it, Viv? I mean, if you suddenly know it's never going to work, surely it's better to break your word, for the other one's sake as well as your own?"

"Of course," said Vivian, stoutly, "but, it's not like you to change your mind easily, is it? There must have been jolly good reasons. You don't have to tell me about it unless you want, it'll keep, for one of those sessions like we used to have, remember? When you're in the mood to let your hair down."

"It's all right," said Asta. "I'm glad I told you. Mind, I haven't had a lot of sympathy over it. Most of Dick's friends think I've been a bitch, to have led him nearly up to the altar and then drop him for no apparent reason. Not even my mother was wholly sympathetic. She liked Dick, just as everyone else did. I haven't been able to talk about it to anyone before. I imagine everyone must think I'm just shallow and changeable. Poor Dick is still going around with a suffering expression. He's even been calling on Mummy, with flowers. It makes me feel awful, I can tell you."

"What went wrong?"

"I knew there *was* something wrong with our relationship. I don't really believe in the passionate love you read about — at least, I don't think I do. It was after I met Dick's parents, and saw how down-trodden and disregarded his mother was. I could see myself getting like that in a few year's time. The worst of it was, Dick couldn't see it himself. He and his father have a positively Eastern attitude towards women. They think we're just there to serve and look after them."

"Doesn't sound like you," agreed Vivian.

"Looking back," said Asta, "I can't help feeling that being a nurse was one of the reasons Dick wanted to marry me. Not that he wanted me to carry on working after we were married, he said so, in fact he was so jealous he'd like to have insisted that I only nursed women patients. I don't think Dick had any appreciation of all the years' slog that went into getting one's SRN badge."

"A right chauvinist," said Vivian, angrily. "You did the right thing, Asta, no doubt about that."

"I expect he thought my training might come in useful if he had a stomach-ache," said Asta, with a watery smile. "If I ever do marry anyone, after that, it's just got to be a man who respects the nursing profession."

"Like a doctor?" asked Vivian, slyly. "Remember we used to think that marrying a doctor was something really fabulous?"

"Maybe," said Asta. "It would be nice to be a help to one's husband, apart from just running the house."

"There are several quite dishy ones at St Margaret's now," said Vivian, kicking off her shoes and waggling her toes luxuriously. "There's Damian Stone, the anaesthetist — six feet one and a shock of Norse fair hair. He's a terrible dancer, though. I got him three times at the last hospital dance, and I was hobbling around the ward for days afterwards. Not too keen on the opposite sex, I'd say. I'm sure he thought I was a different girl each time we danced. I had the feeling I ought to have been wearing red feathers in my hair, or something. Not much to say, either. The usual 'Do you like nursing?'

'Which ward are you on?' and 'Do you play tennis?'"

"Sounds a bit of a bore," said Asta.

"When he said it in the same exact words every time he danced with me, I felt sure there must be a button at the back of his neck that would switch him over to another programme," she answered, wrinkling her nose. "Pity, though, he's quite something to look at."

"Looks," said Asta, with conviction, "are the last thing that matters. That was one of the things I discovered about Dick. Full of a sort of superficial charm, but if a man can bore you when you're engaged, what's he going to be like in ten – twenty years' time?"

"Still," said Vivian, "Damian has got a nice little sailing-boat that he keeps on the Isle of Wight. Bembridge, I think. His parents live there. Verity was asked there for a weekend, and she says it was super. Perhaps he's one of those men who can talk of nothing but boats. Personally, I don't know port from starboard. Maybe he's just shy of girls, and doesn't know what to say to them."

"Could be," said Asta, her thoughts obviously elsewhere. "I'll keep him in mind. You haven't changed a bit, you know, Viv. Always trying to act the marriage broker. What about your own love life? Don't tell me no one has proposed to you. I always thought you look super in your uniform."

Showing a perfect set of teeth in a wide smile, Vivian said "A few from patients, naturally. An occupational hazard, they say. Men are always so vulnerable when they're confined to bed. One from a medical student."

"Oh!" Asta looked interested. "Was there something wrong with him?"

"I couldn't quite see myself going back to Uganda with him. He was very black indeed. Nice chap, though. He married one of the black nurses eventually. Much more suitable. Anyway, the man I marry will have to top my five feet eleven at least another inch."

"Either that, or you'll find some nice little bloke who'll come up to your shoulder," teased Asta. "It's a law of nature."

Next morning, after her first night on duty, Asta sat down to write up her diary.

30 April. 'My first night on duty, and I feel simply flattened. Intend to keep up my diary, though. I feel it's a sort of therapy for me, writing down all the thoughts I couldn't possibly give voice to, even Vivian.

'They really are so terribly short of staff at St Margaret's. I'm glad to be here, really. It's like helping an old friend in trouble, somehow. I'm in charge of four wards, all of them with pretty sick patients, and only one second-year nurse on each. I was trotting to and fro all night. Night Sister Luckham, "Lucky" was on duty, and we did manage to get about ten minutes together and drink a cup of coffee in the duty room. She was really delighted to see me, and rather flatteringly relieved.

'The bug that's been going around the hospital seems to be weakening at last, they've tracked it down to source, Lucky says, a carrier in the kitchen.

'I met quite a few old friends at breakfast, and Vivian has a room quite near to mine. It's like old times to have her popping in and out.

'I phoned Mummy as soon as I came off duty this morning. She and Jim are going to marry by special licence, next week. I'm pleased. At least she won't be lonely now. I'm sure they'll be happy together, Jim's a darling.

'Mummy tells me that Larry has joined the drama club and is making himself very useful. I haven't seen him around the hospital so far, but did bump into Jack Ribstone, who inevitably, used to be called "Pippin". He's a bit like an apple to look at, too, all rosy and round, though I must admit he's a lot thinner than he used to be. We used to go to the cinema together and hold hands in the back row, though it never went any further than that.

'I must have changed a lot since then, too. Anyway, Jack goggled at me when we met in the canteen, and said "My God! If it isn't little Asta. What a stunner you've grown to be. What are you doing on your day off? I've just taken delivery of a new Mini Metro. What about a trial run to the coast?" Said I'd let him know, he's so full of fun and good humour. Not Dick's sort of humour — drier, and a lot more subtle. Might be just what I need. There's no sense in making a hermit of myself, after all.

'Mummy also told me that Dick had called (again). I wish he'd give up, and realise that it's all over, but I think he's too vain to accept it. Now that I'm away from home, I feel more certain than ever I could never have married him.

'I was sitting in the lounge this morning, when I overheard some of

106

the new student nurses discussing one of the doctors.

'He looked straight into my eyes," one of the prettiest ones said. "And I'm sure the way he touched my hand when I handed Mrs Robinson's temperature chart was no accident."

'All the others laughed at her. "Doctor Groves looks everyone straight in the eye," someone said. "But he's only interested in his patients. You're kidding yourself, Eve."

'Then I realised they were talking about Larry. So he's not interested in girls? It would be fun to find out exactly how long he could keep that up if one really tried. That "big strong silent" ploy is sometimes just that, and an inexperienced girl might easily fall for it.

'I'm yawning all over the place, it's time I put my diary away and got into bed. I must say the beds here are the height of luxury. At last they've realised a nurse who spends so much time making other people's beds doesn't want to have to make her own. They've provided us with really splendid duvets, or rather, Vivian tells me, an Arab who was nursed here did. A much more imaginative gift than a silver rose bowl, or even a new operating table!

3 May. What a night! There was an awful accident on the Purley by-pass late in the evening. A mini-bus ran into another car, and there was a slight fog, causing several other cars to pile up behind them. Every available nurse was called. It was a red alert, and we all flew over to the casualty department.

'It was a real shambles, three dead, and at least a dozen badly hurt. St Margaret's was built to cope with that sort of thing, of course, but not with such a skeleton staff.

'I'd been handing clamps and instruments to a pair of hands for some time before I realised they belonged to Larry Groves. I still say he's a very efficient surgeon. After we'd finished, and the last patient had been wheeled away to bed, he took off his mask, and I could see how tired he looked. He was only on call for emergencies, and probably hadn't slept since the night before. It was dawn by then, and as we stepped outside the birds were singing, and pale pink and green hues had appeared on the sky-line.

'He saw me as far as the door of the Home, then said, "Thank you, Asta." He seemed as though he wanted to say something more, but turned abruptly and went away.

'I'm beginning to find my rudeness to him on the morning when I scraped my car, through sheer cussedness on my part, as I realise now, more and more stupid. I can only imagine it was so soon after breaking my engagement with Dick, and I was upset. Larry was so friendly and helpful to start with, but he's now extremely chilly. It wouldn't have hurt me to at least be polite, especially after the way he's helped Mummy with all those little jobs. There was no excuse for being so very bitchy, and I suppose he thinks

I'm a spoiled brat.

'Maybe I am. After all, Mummy has always run around after me, and I've taken it all for granted. It's her wedding on Friday, and I have two nights off. There's to be a small reception at the Bear and Tipstaff, mostly her friends from the drama club, so I shall go and help. She and Jim are going to Paris for a week, and Mummy seemed so happy when I phoned her. I suppose I'd better put this diary away until after the wedding, I shan't have much time for writing in it. I've offered to write all the "thank you" letters for Mummy. She's had some super presents — one is apt not to notice how popular one's mother is.

8 May. 'Mummy and Jim have left on their honeymoon, and I'm back at St Margaret's. It's no use, I must write it down in my diary, since I can't tell anyone, not even Viv. Thank goodness it's rather a super sort of diary, a birthday present from Jim. It has a lock and key, so there's no fear of anyone's reading it.

'I feel so exhilarated, and yet so miserable. I'm in love. Not any kind of love I could have imagined. It's like going into a great cathedral, lit by beautiful stained-glass windows. Somewhere in the back there's an organ playing Bach. First a gentle whisper of music, then, the player pulls out all the stops and the place is full of unbelievable music, harmonies you've never heard before.

'It's no use putting your fingers in your ears, and pretending you can't hear it — the music is inside you, filling every part.

'That old term "playing on your heart-strings" has been used over and over until it's just a cliché. Now it has a new meaning for you.

'To think I told Mummy I didn't like his name. I love the sound of it now. I must have been crazy to have been so beastly to him. I'm terrified I shall never be able to put his impression of me right. How thankful I am it was all over with Dick before I even met Larry. He's the sort of man who'd never look at another man's girl.

'How can I find words to describe my love for him? I only know I'd follow him, wherever he went — if only he'd let me.

'I've tried to remember the precise moment when I knew I was in love with Larry. Perhaps when I saw the way he cared about that little cat?

'No, I think it was at Mummy's wedding — yes, I'm sure it was. He was there, of course, doing all sorts of things for Mummy, looking after the guests. He was quite polite to me, and seeing him alone for a moment, I went up and said "Thank you for everything you've done, Larry. I also saw you had sprayed the paintwork on my car. It was very nice of you, and I'm sorry I was so rude about it that morning."

'He just looked over the top of my head, and waved to someone in the reception room and said in a very off-hand voice, "It only took me a few minutes. You were quite right, I shouldn't have interfered. Only the rust would have started if it hadn't been covered."

'Then he said "Excuse me, Asta," and went off leaving me standing there, feeling I'd been ticked off for not taking the Mini to a garage.

'Then one of the guests, a niece of Jim's called Eve started to feel a bit groggy. Too much champagne, I imagine, so I took her to a little side room one of the waiters showed me. He brought us some tea, and I sat with her on a little settee by the window, which I opened for some fresh air. It had got rather stuffy in the reception room, and I was glad to get away for a while.

'Then Larry put his head round the door. I suppose someone who knew he is a doctor had told him about Eve.

'"I think she'd better be taken home," he said, "I'll go and call a taxi." He came back after a few minutes, and helped Eve out of the room.

'I'd had several glasses of champagne myself, and not too much to eat with it, being busy helping with the guests. It was so cool and comfortable in the little room, so quiet after the noisy reception. I put my head back on a cushion and closed my eyes for a few moments. They wouldn't miss me for a while, I thought, sleepily.

'I must have dropped off pretty quickly — thinking it was only for a few minutes, but to my dismay, when I woke I could see the daylight was fading outside. Then Larry came again, calling my name, and I jumped to my feet, startled. He strode over to me, looking quite angry, I thought.

'"I wondered where on earth you were," he said, coming over to where I stood. "All the guests have gone home."

'Still feeling half asleep, and a bit woozy, I staggered a bit, and fell up against Larry's chest.

'It was the strangest thing. I don't remember how I came to be in his arms, but his lips were on mine. It was a bitter, ruthless sort of kiss on his part, almost as though it was against his will. It was over in a minute, and he let go of me.

'"I'm sorry," he said, "I shouldn't have done that. Are you all right now?"

'I held on to his arm. I only knew I wanted his kiss to go on for ever. He'd held me so close against his jacket I could feel the thud of his heart. No need to tell a nurse that his pulse was quicker than it should have been.

'Yet, as he released me, and I looked up into his face, I was shocked at Larry's expression. So hard, his mouth so grim, it made me flare up.

'"I don't know why you bothered to kiss me," I said, stormily, "you obviously didn't enjoy it." Then I ran out of the room, tears of anger running down my cheeks. Yes, that must have been the moment I knew I loved him.

'My own car was outside in the park,

and I was absolutely sober now. I drove off, my cheeks flaming, but an icy cold feeling in my heart.

'I know it serves me right. Larry must think I'm the kind of girl who can break off an engagement one week and find someone else the next. I can understand that, too, but how could I possibly have anticipated falling in love so soon?

'When I think of how that reception might have been for my own wedding to Dick. I fell quite sick with relief that it wasn't. Dick was at the wedding. I suppose Mummy must have asked him. I don't think she's quite given up hope I might change my mind again and marry him after all. Dick didn't really make a nuisance of himself, but he did put on a hearty sort of "let's be friends" act.

'I caught Larry looking at us once or twice, a bit puzzled, I think. Dick insisted on our having a drink together. Perhaps Larry imagined I'd just invited Dick in order to gloat, or something.

I certainly don't seem to let Larry see me in good light.

'Things are getting back to normal at St Margaret's now. Most of the staff are back on their jobs, so I suppose Mrs Adams will be wanting me to move on to something else.

'I lay awake thinking over the problem of whether to tell them I'd like to stay on at St Margaret's on a permanent basis. At least I should see Larry sometimes, even work with him. It would be better than nothing. I don't want to go back to living at home, not just yet, anyway, however nice Jim is, they'll want to be alone for a while.

15 May. 'Mrs Adams sent me my cheque this morning, and wants to see me, so I suppose this is it. I don't know how much longer I shall stay here, but it's going to be an awful wrench leaving St Margaret's and all my friends. Especially Vivian, I shall miss her a lot.

'She came in last night with a story that Larry is leaving England altogether,

and going back to Australia. What shall
I do? What shall I do? Perhaps it's
sort of punishment for my treatment
of Dick?

25 May. 'I haven't had the heart to
write in my diary lately. It is true,
Larry is going back to Australia, in a
fortnight's time. Someone came round
with a box for subscriptions, to give
him a farewell party. He's very popular.
I just want to die.'

5

MRS ADAMS smiled ingratiatingly at Asta, who immediately felt somewhat wary.

"Sit down, Asta," she said. "How was it at St Margaret's? Hectic, I expect. I had a nice letter in the post this morning from the senior nursing officer, saying how much she appreciated your help, especially during the emergency, recently."

"Thank you," said Asta, taking a seat in front of Mrs Adams's desk "I did what I could, naturally — that's the whole object of one's training, isn't it? Actually, I'm enjoying my duties at St Margaret's, it's just like old times, meeting friends. In fact, Mrs Adams, I'm seriously thinking of taking up — "

Mrs Adams, sensing what was coming, jumped in quickly. "I have a very attractive proposition to make to you, Asta. A plum job that you deserve. I thought of you at once, you're just the right girl for it!"

Mrs Adams wasn't the woman to hand out compliments unless she had a very good reason. Asta watched the firm, precise mouth suspiciously. Something was brewing and she was the main ingredient in the pot. She gave herself a little shake. No one, not even Mrs Adams could persuade her to do something she wouldn't like. She'd practically made up her mind to tell the woman she intended to sign on at St Margaret's permanently. Everyone had been so nice, and now that Mummy no longer needed her to be home every evening, it would be a good proposition.

Mrs Adams was carefully arranging all the little objects on her desk — like someone playing war games with toy soldiers. Then she came out with her salvo.

"How would you like a trip to Australia,

Asta?" she asked, triumphantly. "I've never sent one of my nurses so far before, but this is a very special case. You'd be accompanying one small girl, that's all. A real rest after your work at St Margaret's. Have you had much experience of flying?"

"No Mrs Adams," said Asta firmly, "just a couple of flights to the Channel Islands, that's all. To tell you the truth, I'm not terribly keen on flying, I much prefer the sea."

Asta's voice was listless, totally uninterested in the project. "I'm sure there are plenty of other nurses who'd jump at the chance."

Ordinarily, *she'd* have jumped at the chance, Asta knew. It was something she'd dreamed of in the past. But today, all her thoughts kept going to the fact that Larry would be leaving England soon, for good, probably. Go away and leave her, carrying her regret that she hadn't been even decently polite to him. She'd thought so often about the way he'd kissed her, at the wedding. Why had he? Perhaps he had been just trying her out, to see whether she would flirt with any man who came across her path? The warm blood flooded her cheeks as she remembered the way she'd clung to Larry, responded to his kiss.

Even if she took this job in Australia, she'd only be there for a short while, probably before flying home again. She couldn't see the vaguest chance she'd meet Larry there. Why should she? It might be embarrassing even if she did come across him. Maybe he'd think she was running after him.

Asta tightened her resolve. She still had her pride, however much she loved him. She'd always had the men after her, not the other way round.

Mrs Adams's voice, friendly but firm, was going on somewhere — getting a little impatient, though. "All expenses paid, naturally, Asta, and a very good bonus into the bargain. I can't imagine why you should hesitate."

Asta shrugged. "I expect you think

I'm being stupid, Mrs Adams, but I really don't care for flying very much. Even if it was Concorde we were going to Australia in."

"The plane you'd be flying in is a private aircraft, part-owned by Mr Crane — little Vida's father. He only takes about ten passengers on each trip. The rest of the plane is for goods, he told me. He's very anxious I should find the right nurse to accompany his daughter, and he really wants you, especially."

"Why me?" asked Asta, curiously.

"You know I keep a file of all my nurses, with photographs?"

"Yes, of course, I gave you one of mine, didn't I?"

"Little Vida recognised you at once, and said 'That's the nurse I want. She was on night duty when I was in the hospital. She used to tell me stories when I couldn't sleep.' You remember little Vida? Reddish curls, and enormous grey eyes. A most engaging child, I thought. Her father thinks the world of her — nothing is too good."

"Yes, of course, I remember Vida, a lovely little girl, not a bit spoiled."

Mrs Adams riffled through a file of papers in front of her.

"They are staying with his sister while they're in England. Perhaps you'd like to go and see them? The plane will be ready to leave in a few day's time. It's gone to Amsterdam to pick up some cargo, Mr Crane told me. What do you say, Asta? Surely you can't refuse such a golden opportunity to see the world, at no cost to yourself, either."

Studying Asta's face, she said "I think it would do you good. You know, my dear, you've been working too hard. Mr Crane said that if you fancied staying over in Sydney for a holiday after your nursing duties are over, he'd welcome the idea. I rather think he'd like your advice about getting another nurse after you've gone. Vida will need attention for some time to come. He'd send you back by private plane at any time you wish."

"He certainly sounds pretty well-off," said Asta.

"I would imagine their life style to be lavish," smiled Mrs Adams, "it would be a wonderful holiday for you, Asta. Mr Crane phoned again this morning, asking me to do my best to persuade you. The child's quite set on having you, and not some other nurse."

"I remember Vida," said Asta. "Some malformation of the feet, wasn't it? I did wonder why she'd been brought to England, when there are very good hospitals in Australia. She didn't sleep very well. I did wonder whether there's anything in the theory that going from one side of the world to the other so quickly might upset the sleep rhythms. There wasn't a lot of time for telling her stories, but I used to manage a few minutes sometimes. A dear little soul, and no trouble."

"Mr Crane is an Englishman who went out to Australia when he was a young man," said Mrs Adams. "He had reason to remember St Margaret's hospital, he told me, and nothing but the best would do for his only child."

"Is there a mother?" asked Asta.

"He didn't mention one. I got the impression she was either dead or divorced."

"He sounds like a man who'd be willing to pay for *anything* he wanted," said Asta. "I don't know that I like the sound of him very much."

"He's very nice, really," said Mrs Adams, eagerly, "just a little over-protective to Vida, that's all. He's willing to pay whatever it costs for Vida to have the right nurse to accompany her home, then stay for at least a fortnight to get the child really well again. The holiday he offers afterwards will be entirely separate, naturally. You'll be a very silly girl to refuse such an offer, Asta, believe me."

A distrustful feeling was still in Asta's mind. Mrs Adams's fee must have been an extremely good one to make her so enthusiastic and affable. Maybe she *was* being a bit unreasonable after all. A trip abroad might stop her brooding over Larry. Stop that awful ache in her heart every time she saw a tall man in a white coat whisking through the hospital.

While Asta still hesitated, Mrs Adams consulted her notes once more. "A doctor from St Margaret's will be travelling on the same plane, Asta. He's promised to keep an eye on you and the child, see you through Customs, and so on."

Asta's mouth was dry, and she could hardly control the trembling of lips as she said, "A doctor, Mrs Adams? Travelling to Sydney?"

If only it could be Larry. It had to be Larry. In a few seconds her mind had gone through all the possible doctors at St Margaret's — none of them fitted. Anyway, wasn't Larry going home?

"Do you know which doctor?" she asked, trying to appear nonchalant, but firmly crossing her fingers — something she hadn't done since schooldays.

"Dear St Jude, patron of hopeless causes," she prayed, "please let it be Larry."

At least she would have his company on the plane; he couldn't very well avoid her and little Vida, after promising to help. Besides, he was so good with children.

Mrs Adams was looking through the papers with infuriating slowness. At last she said "Yes, er, let me see. A Doctor Laurence Groves. You know him Asta? He appears to be a friend of the Crane family in Sydney, so naturally was offered a seat in the plane."

"I see," said Asta, her heart bounding with gratitude, "Yes, of course I know Doctor Groves. It will be nice to be travelling with him."

If Mrs Adams was surprised at Asta's sudden change of mind, she said nothing, but her voice sounded relieved. If Mrs Adams's face could be said to go so far, she beamed.

"That's right, there's a sensible girl. The rest of the passengers are employees of Mr Crane's business, he tells me. The trip was arranged for them, a sort of bonus for long service. Altogether a most generous man, wouldn't you say, Asta?"

She paused. "Are you listening, Asta?"

Asta shook herself out of the rosy dream she was having. Surely fate must be having a hand in this. She forced herself to listen to Mrs Adams, who was going on about passports, inoculations, warnings.

"That's it then, Asta. Oh! I nearly forgot — " She unclipped a small pink piece of paper from a letter. "Mr Crane left a cheque for £250, to buy whatever clothes, or travelling luggage you might need. He told me not to forget to tell you, it will be winter in Sydney when you arrive, so bring some nice thick woollies and a warm coat."

Feeling a little dazed, Asta put the cheque into her handbag. "£250 for clothes?" she asked, "This must be an advance on salary, of course."

"But no, indeed," came the reply, "Mr Crane explained that it was a gesture to pay for the rush, a sort of compensation. I'm sure you need have no compunction about taking it. He can plainly afford it."

"I feel I'd rather buy my clothes myself," said Asta, "but I must admit that funds are a bit low after Mummy's wedding present, and I'll be glad of a loan."

"Well," shrugged Mrs Adams, "that's something you'll have to sort out later with Mr Crane, won't you? He's a very persuasive gentleman, as well as being a very rich one."

"Will he be travelling with us?" asked Asta, "I do hope he won't be fussing over Vida all the time."

"No, he can't travel back with you and the child, as he has some urgent business to attend to, but he'll be back in Sydney shortly after you arrive. He did ask if you'd call and see him. He's staying with a sister in Welwyn Garden City while in England. If you could go up there, it's only a train journey of about twenty miles or so. Just to fill in the details. Here's the address."

"I'm off duty tomorrow," said Asta, "I'll go then. I know the Garden City quite well."

"Once you reach Sydney, you'll have no problems, Asta. Mr Crane assures me you will be met on the airfield and taken straight to his home. It's in the best part of Sydney, Rose Bay, overlooking the harbour. You'll love it, Asta. I quite envy you, looking after one small girl will be easy after the past few weeks at St Margaret's won't it?"

Smiling her thanks, Asta tried to look cool and collected. Inside, her brain was furiously asking questions to which only time could ever give an answer. But at least she wasn't saying 'goodbye' to Larry for a while. This was only a respite, but it gave a glimmer of hope that she might at least be seen doing her own responsible job, looking after a sick child, and maybe erase some of the unfortunate image she had given Larry.

She wouldn't have to say 'goodbye' to him in a crowded room, with all the other nurses making eyes at him.

"Goodbye, and thank you, Mrs Adams," she said. "I'll see you when I come back, of course."

Next day, with the cheque safely in her bank, Asta went shopping with Vivian, who'd some time off. Her friend had been almost stricken dumb when Asta told her of the trip to Sydney. "Gosh!" she said, her round blue eyes wide with envy. "I'd give anything for a chance like that."

"It certainly does seem a bit unbelievable," agreed Asta, "and I almost turned it down at first."

Vivian was too engrossed in the display of clothes in a store window to question why Asta could have thought of anything so crazy.

"Mrs Adams told me to take plenty of woollies," said Asta, "I always thought Australia was very hot, didn't you, Viv?"

"Not in winter," said Vivian, "I

spent two years there with my parents, when I was a kid. It can be really chilly in the evenings. Even some days it's bitterly cold. Not all the time, though. There are some beautiful winter days when it's warm enough to swim. Of course, the water never gets really cold out there. Wait until you see some of their life savers. Great bronzed giants of men. Lots of the girls just sit on the beaches, drooling. Don't fall for one of them, though, Asta. They spend all their leisure time training, and their wives, if they've ever taken the time off to get married, hardly ever see them."

"No fear of that, I promise you," said Asta. "I rather like the look of that blue stripey dress on the model, don't you? Let's go inside, there are a lot of nice things in the window, but they're all for summer, aren't they?"

"They must have woollies inside," said Vivian, "it's no use pretending we don't need them here, even in June."

Asta chose a periwinkle blue suit in fine wool, several chunky sweaters, and still had a nice little sum in hand.

"I'd better have a long dress," she said. "I don't know what the set-up will be at the Crane's house, but both my evening dresses are a bit tatty after several hospital dances. I suppose I shan't be allowed much luggage on the plane?" she asked. "I'd better get a light-weight suitcase, too."

Asta was determined to look her best on that journey with Larry. She had her hair shaped and set at the store's hairdressing department, and paid the fabulous price without a blink.

In her wardrobe at home were a lot of nice clothes she'd bought for her wedding when she was engaged to Dick, but she knew they would never be worn now. Perhaps the firm she'd bought them from would exchange them. Dick had been with her when she'd chosen some of the dresses, and they were more to please his taste than hers.

She'd always preferred bright, clear colours, but he had dismissed several things that appealed to her with "Bit showy, darling, aren't they?" No doubt she'd have ended up as a drab little mouse in greys and browns after a short while, like his mother.

Choosing an evening dress in a vivid flame colour, she recognised, with an inward grin, that a psychologist would tell her she was casting off the last of Dick's domination.

It would be difficult to imagine Larry even going into a dress shop with her, let alone trying to tell her what to buy.

Waiting for Asta's purchases to be wrapped, Vivian asked, "Did you volunteer for this job in Australia, Asta? Who wouldn't?" she said hastily, "If they were free to take it, but I've wondered a bit about it, you know. You don't look over the moon, as you should be at such a super chance. Not having second thoughts about that broken engagement, are you? I should think that going to your mother's wedding must have been a bit unsettling."

Asta shook her head. "No, Viv. No regrets on that score, I do assure you. I'm only too grateful it was all over before . . . What I felt for Dick wasn't love, I know that now. It would have been total disaster to have married him. Not that I wouldn't have worked at it, and I suppose that so long as I didn't expect too much, it might have worked as well as most marriages do."

Vivian gave her a searching look, I have the feeling that someone else has turned up; am I right? Yes, I can see he has — you never were any good at disguising things from me, you know, Asta. Are all these new clothes for him? I'm dying to know. Did you know him before you broke off with Dick, and was that the reason for it?"

Asta hastily disclaimed the notion. "No, it wasn't at all like that, Viv. I had met Larry a number of times before I broke it off with Dick, but he wasn't anything to do with it. Far from being in love with him, I found him rather infuriating at first. He tried

136

to be friendly and helpful, and I was rude to him — terribly rude. It makes me go hot all over whenever I think of it, no wonder he can't stand the sight of me now."

"When did you know, about being in love with him, I mean?"

"It was a sort of revelation. It was just as though there was a corner of my heart that had been empty and waiting for him to come. A secret place where no one had ever been before — a place even I didn't know existed. And I had to spoil it all by acting like a silly kid. Maybe I was just afraid to let my emotions take over, after the affair with Dick, putting up a sort of defensive barrier, in case it happened again. Now it's probably too late — he just looks over the top of my head."

"H'm," said Vivian, looking at her friend's trim figure, beautiful eyes, and the newly styled golden cap of hair shining in the sunlight, "I find that hard to believe. They say any girl can get any man if she really wants him, and with your advantages, it should be a walk-over."

Then her bantering tone became serious. "He isn't married, is he, old girl? I know what your opinion of girls who break up married couples is, but — well, if it's not a happy one?"

"No," said Asta, miserably, "it isn't that at all."

"Don't tell me he hasn't shown any interest," said Vivian, scornfully, "there must be something wrong with a man like that."

"He did kiss me, at Mummy's wedding, but it was as though he didn't really want to, as though he's regretted it immediately afterwards. It gave me a shaken ego, I can tell you, having a man turn to stone in my arms. He boards with Mrs Biggs, next door to my home. She's a terrible gossip, stands behind the curtains and sees everyone's coming and going. I wonder if she could have told Larry something awful about me."

"Such as what?" Vivian's eyes were curious.

"Maybe she thinks I'm still keeping Dick on a string. She told Mummy that he called one day when we were both out, and she had asked him in for a cup of tea. He used to board with Mrs Biggs when he was a student. That's how we met, as a matter of fact. Dick thinks if he keeps on long enough, I'm bound to give in and marry him after all. He's too vain to realise it's really over between us. Dick can be a real charmer when he wants. He even had Mummy on his side — she was very fond of him. I was too, I'll admit, but I know now what a frightful mistake it would have been. Even if I die an old maid," she said, between clenched teeth, "I'll still be glad I didn't marry Dick."

She gave a bitter little laugh. "I even apologised to Larry, for my rudeness, but I don't think it's just that. His attitude has changed towards me, he's almost antagonistic somehow."

"Larry. Larry?" Vivian's tone was a mixture of surprise and delight at having penetrated Asta's secret. "Of course. It must be. Doctor Laurence Groves. It is, isn't it, Asta? He's a really super man, just right for you. I've only just realised. All the kids in the ward call him Doctor Larry. They all adore him — what a waste if he really is a misogynist — not that I believe it."

She leaned over to Asta, and whispered over the enticing music that came over the stores intercom. "I feel it in my bones, old girl, let Gipsy Vivian Walker tell your future. You'll get your man, I'm sure of it. You needn't bother to cross my somewhat hot and sticky little palm with whatever they make 10p pieces with these days. You'll marry your hero, and live happily ever after, see if you don't."

Asta accepted her parcels from the assistant with a smile. "I wish I could rely on that, Viv," she said, "but at least I'll have this trip to Australia. I wish it had been by sea. I could have had a month or more with him. I shall just have to make the most of it, that's all."

"I've often thought I'd have a go at writing a novel," said Vivian, with a gleam in her eye. "One with a hospital background. I'll make you the heroine — and of course, it'll have a happy ending, that goes without saying."

The smile hovering around Asta's full lips was wistful. "I shall write it all down in my diary, I've always kept one, since I was at school. Everything he says, it'll be some sort of comfort to me when I have to come back to England without him. But I'm not even going to let myself think about leaving him there. There simply has to be a way of getting through to him that I'm not the rude, conceited, changeable idiot he seems to imagine me."

"Who does he think he is?" demanded Vivian, aggressively. "He can't know you as I do. Why you're one of the most dependable people I know. Didn't anyone ever tell him that any girl with an SRN badge has to be? He simply doesn't know you at all."

Asta shrugged, "No, and he's made it fairly plain he doesn't intend to, either. He'll jolly well be forced to speak to me on the plane, after telling Vida's father he'd look after us."

★ ★ ★

Next day, after a short train journey to where Mr Crane and his daughter were staying, Asta was greeted with enthusiasm by the little girl. He was a typical businessman to look at, she thought, of medium height, but appearing taller by the way he held every inch of him to the best advantage. Piercing dark eyes with heavy brows, sparse grey hair dragged over a balding head. Asta was to discover that he rarely spoke first, appearing to enjoy summing others up by their speech and movements. At any rate, Asta seemed to pass. Little Vida was bubbling over with excitement, red-golden curls bobbing as she hung on to Asta's hand. She was beginning to walk again after the plastic surgery on her feet, which had had a slight malformation from birth.

"You're not going to leave me again as soon as we get home, are you Asta?" she asked, pleadingly.

Mr Crane made an apologetic murmur. "You must ask Nurse Milne if she minds your using her Christian name, dear," he said. "Perhaps she would rather you didn't?"

"Not at all," said Asta, warming to the child at once. "I'm surprised at her remembering it. She did ask me what it was one night at the hospital."

"Your plane will leave London Airport at ten o'clock on Wednesday morning," he said. "Everything will be arranged for you both. You know that my friend Doctor Groves will be on the plane, and a friend of his, too, Kenneth Markham. He knows that one of the nurses from St Margaret's will be with Vida, but when I saw him last I wasn't sure whether you'd be taking the job, so I didn't mention your name. You know him, I take it?"

"Yes," said Asta, sipping her tea, and trying to hide the sudden colour in her cheeks at the mere sound of Larry's name.

"A car will pick you up at the hospital in time to catch the plane, and Vida will be in it with my sister. Ah! here she is. Rachel, my dear, this is Nurse Asta Milne, who will be accompanying Vida, so now you can stop worrying about that."

Rachel's pixie face broke into smiles as she greeted Asta. "My brother might have made his way in the world," she said, with a fond glance in his direction, "but he's still my baby brother. It was so lovely to see them both."

She smiled at Asta, "my little niece here is a little subdued by her operation, but you'll find her quite a handful now she's well again. I've packed a small bag with some games, and a few books, you might find them handy on the trip — she'll need to be amused."

"Thank you," said Asta, "I expect we shall be glad of them."

So, evidently it was all settled in everybody's minds. On Wednesday she'd be on her way. There would be a job to do, looking after little Vida, but there *must* be some stray moments when the child would be asleep, when, surely, Larry could hardly avoid talking to her, however mundane the conversation.

6

MR CRANE'S eyes went to the magnificent bunch of red roses that had just been delivered to the plane. "Well, well," he said, with a tight little smile, "someone thinks a lot of our little nurse, eh?"

Asta accepted the flowers with a smile, and hope in her heart — then after looking at the card that had come with them, pushed them aside. "Bon voyage, my darling, come back soon, I'll be waiting. Dick."

It wasn't an auspicious start, was it? She could see the other passengers giving her quizzical looks. What an infernal nerve Dick had. Asta couldn't imagine how he'd heard of her going to Australia, with Mummy still away. Yes, of course, that wretched Mrs Biggs next door. Trust her to have heard about it from somewhere, and passed it on to

Dick. He was quite capable of snooping about to find out what she was doing.

Mr Crane was fussing around Vida. "You won't forget, Nurse," he said, "Doctor Groves will be going all the way. Anything you want, anything at all, he's promised to help you with. I shall have to leave now, the plane's due for lift off. Goodbye, my darling," he kissed his little daughter fondly. "I wish I was travelling with you — but I just can't manage it."

Larry, standing nearby, shook hands with him. "Don't worry," he said, "Vida's fine now."

Asta sank into the comfortable seat allocated to her, and fastened Vida's seat belt. They were ingeniously designed seats, she found, after Larry had shown her how to lower them into a comfortable bed when necessary. Complete with subdued light for reading, a bell at hand to summon the stewardess, everything one would be likely to need.

The roses, in their expensive, ribbon-trimmed pack were just an embarrassment. She felt sure she'd never want to smell roses again. However she thrust them down beside her seat, where they were out of sight.

Larry sat nearby, on a seat next to his friend, Ken Markham. She was sure he'd been surprised to see her when he entered the plane; it wouldn't have occurred to him that the nurse from St Margaret's might be she. Maybe he wouldn't have been so quick to offer help if he had known, she thought, a little bitterly.

Ken had been introduced with a brusque "Ken, this is Asta Milne; Asta, Ken Milne, an old friend. Asta is accompanying young Vida here to her home in Sydney. She's a nurse."

Ken looked a nice boy, she thought, and made an instant success with the little girl, who, as soon as the plane was safely in the air, and their seat-belts off, was perched on his knee, full of chatter and questions.

He was soon crooning to her, anything from 'The Campbells are

Coming' to old Aborigine chants, and a Tasmanian war dance that had her in fits of laughter that ended in a bout of hiccoughs. Larry, coming back from talking to one of the stewardesses, took Vida's seat beside Asta, watching Ken and the child's fun with an amused grin.

"Your friend has a beautiful voice," Asta ventured. "One can tell even from his singing to Vida."

"He's a professional singer," said Larry. "Ken's had an offer to join an opera group in Sydney. I'm sure he'll make good — he really deserves to."

When tea was served, Asta half expected Larry would go back to his seat beside Ken, but he made no sign of moving. He looked particularly boyish and handsome in an intricately knitted white sweater and plum-coloured corduroy slacks. She found herself wondering who had knitted the sweater for him — surely it must have been a labour of love. Some woman in Australia? She tried to imagine what sort of woman she might have been, and whether she was waiting for him to go back home to her.

Whoever she is, Asta thought, fiercely, damn her! The most *she'd* ever aspired to was the simplest of knitting patterns, and not always successful at that.

She remembered with a shudder those hideously long operation stockings one of the night sisters had been so keen on their making in the small hours. Enough to put anyone off knitting for life.

"I've been admiring your sweater," she said, at last. "It's so beautifully knitted. Who made it?"

Larry examined the sleeve as though he had only just seen it for the first time. "Oh! A grateful patient. Dear old lady. Rather gorgeous, isn't it?"

"Wonderful!" Asta felt a ridiculous sense of relief. No besotted girl-friend, after all.

Although the plane was so small compared with the modern jumbo jets, or Concorde, it lacked nothing in comfort, she found. The food, cooked in some unseen galley, was practically cordon bleu; the wine, served at just the right temperature, of the finest.

There were two stewardesses, in blue linen uniforms with a gold bird embroidered on the breast pockets. Asta found, with some amusement, that the ornamentation represented a crane. The same bird appeared on the silver table ware, tea-pots, coffee jugs, and was even etched on the crystal glasses. Evidently Mr Crane enjoyed putting his mark on all his possessions.

The little dark stewardess, with beautiful tawny eyes, was named Annie, and the other, a striking Norwegian girl with sleek gold hair, was addressed as Oggie. Asta felt it must be short for something else.

Although Asta had been quite prepared and willing to give the whole of her time to little Vida, it wasn't working out that way at all. The child seemed to be acquainted with all the other people travelling with them, and to be a favourite of everyone.

They all wanted to talk to her, find interesting things in their hand luggage to show her, and generally kept her so amused that Asta hardly saw her for some time.

She'd brought a couple of books with her, as well as her diary, which she was determined to keep up to date. 'Larry is so remote,' she wrote in it, that evening. 'I'm tongue-tied too. I keep starting to say something, then stop, wondering if I'm boring him. He isn't rude, he answers any questions I put to him, but he doesn't really look at me — it's as though there's a glass partition between us.

'I like his friend, Ken, very much. He's being wonderful with Vida. If I get a chance when we reach Sydney, I'd like to hear him sing. The little dark hostess seems very taken with him, hanging around him, giving him special attention, but he just doesn't notice her. I wonder why? He doesn't look like a woman-hater to me.

'Perhaps he and Larry are starting a new club, "Females Anonymous" for men who don't want girls. We won't be allowed to leave the plane when it stops, I'm told. Rather a disappointment, I was looking forward to seeing other places, but it's something to do with the cargo we carry, Larry told me, though he couldn't tell me what it is. I suppose it can't be anything dangerous, or Mr Crane wouldn't have put Vida on it, would he?

'Now and again the pilot's voice comes over the intercom, telling us what we should see if we look out, but we're travelling so high that the clouds are in the way most of the time.

'Perhaps I shall come back home by boat — it would be more interesting. Not that I want to think about that. Not leaving Larry behind, probably for ever. His arm is very close to mine, if I edge a little closer, I can feel the warmth of his body, but *he's* quite unconscious of it, I'm sure. It's a good job I keep my diary in shorthand, or I wouldn't dare to be writing in it now, for fear he should inadvertently see what I've written. I'll write it down, I love you. I love you. What a funny little squiggle it looks in Pitman's. To think I was going to work in an office before I started at St Margaret's. Then I should probably not have met Larry . . . or should I? I suppose he'd still have lodged at Mrs Biggs, next door. Maybe I should have left home at a different time in the mornings, though, and we wouldn't have had that silly scene about the man who parked outside our gate. I suppose I was rude to him because I was so upset about Dick. I'm not usually so bad-tempered, am I?

'They're coming round with another meal now, so I'd better persuade Vida to come and sit up for it. She's certainly having a wonderful time.

'I hope Mummy and Jim are having a lovely honeymoon. They should be on their way home by now. Perhaps I might consider taking a job in Sydney now that she's not alone. But that would seem too much like running after Larry. What to do? I never in my wildest dreams thought of myself in such a position. Has he forgotten when he held me in his arms and kissed me? From the way he's acting now, I might be some frumpish female he's just met on the plane!' She closed her diary wearily.

Soon after dinner, Vida's heavy head began to nod, so Asta took her to the well-equipped bathroom, changed her into her nightie, and when she came back, found that Larry had extended the seat to make a comfortable bed. She tucked the child up with her favourite teddy, and watched her fall asleep almost at once.

Larry and Ken, with a small table slotted between them were engrossed in a game of chess by the time she'd finished, totally occupied with their game.

Asta pretended to be reading, though the words were not making any imprint on her brain. The minutes spent so close to Larry were too precious to be wasted.

Leaning back on her cushion, Asta could almost close her eyes and still keep the two men in vision. Larry with his red hair glowing warmly in the overhead lights. She was able to study him more closely than she'd ever dared before through her thick eyelashes. The way his ears were set close to his head, his jawline, firm and strong, the tiny gold hairs on the backs of his hands. There was a small scar at the base of one of his thumbs that she'd not noticed before. She wondered how it had come there. Big, capable hands they were, in contrast to Ken's rather small white ones. Well kept, with the nails pared short — a real man's hands.

She wanted, with a terrible longing, to be part of his life, to know everything that had happened to him. How could there be any future without Larry? She yearned to feel his hands touch her, caress her. It was almost too much, being so close to him, maddening to see him so engrossed in his game of chess with Ken. Poor Ken, she almost felt jealous of him. What a fool she was. She'd just got to make a better show than this, take hold of herself. She wandered up the gangway, speaking to some of the other passengers. There were six of them beside Larry, Vida, Ken and herself. She'd met them all, during the day.

Directly behind her seat was a man she'd immediately dubbed the amorous prawn in her mind.

A round, pink little man of fifty years or so, with sparse, pale bristly whiskers and protuberant little black eyes, and hands that might well have been feelers from the way they managed to touch any attractive female within his reach. His name, Asta learned with some amusement, was Jack Salmon ('They call me Sammy') and he was chief sales representative for one of Mr Crane's interests, a plastics factory.

He'd had a marvellous year, he told everyone who'd listen, sold more of Mr Crane's products than anyone before or since. This trip he'd had to 'the smoke' was a bonus.

He spoke in a penetrating, high-pitched voice, a curious mixture of Australian and Cockney slang, continually looking around to see what effect his somewhat dubious jokes were having on everyone else, and consuming as many large glasses of beer as he could persuade the stewardess to bring.

Judging from the flash in the Norwegian girl's eyes when his hand closed over hers every time she handed him his drink, Asta thought, amused, one of them is going to land in his lap.

On the seat beside him was a giant of a man, more than half Aborigine, from the darkness of his skin and the thickness of his lips, but having some white blood that had given him eyes of a beautiful azure blue. Like a sailor's eyes, used to looking into the distance.

A gentle soul, Asta found, with the patience to listen to his neighbour's boring tales, nodding and smiling at the right places, which was all 'Sammy' needed to go on, and on, and on.

All the rest of the plane's passengers soon knew of his adventures — the girls he'd met and conquered during his vacation, the ones he was going back to in Sydney.

In the seat behind them were two women, both with the high, rather unattractive voices of the average Australian woman. Each had large bags of knitting wool and needles, and might have been sitting at home in front of the fire for all the notice they took of anyone else. The one on the left was Mrs Munt, a crisp, fresh-faced little person whose sole contribution to the conversation was "There now" or "Wouldn't it?".

Asta soon found that this last meant either "Wouldn't it surprise you?" "Wouldn't it be a good thing?" or "Wouldn't it be a pity?", according to the one in which it was delivered.

The other knitter, Mrs Murdoch, who, with one long needle tucked under her arm in the fashion of the Arran Isle knitters, worked so fast that the jumper grew visibly under her fingers, had more to say. Mrs Murdoch would have been quite handsome but for a slightly feline look about the thin mouth, and a way of peering with bright green eyes, eyes that seemed not to refer to the work in her hands, but to be fixed with a basilisk look on some invisible screen.

Asta's impression was justified when after tea, she offered to read the tea-leaves in Mrs Munt's cup.

"Turn it around three times," she said, "then put it down on the saucer until it drains out." The catlike eyes peered into the cup, turned it round and round in her thin fingers, then she gave a little grunt. The other passengers, looking on with amusement, smiled politely or burst into laughter, according to their natures, when Mrs Murdoch, in a deep voice entirely unlike her usual one said, "I see a long journey."

"Not exactly an inspired guess," joked Ken, "seeing we're about half way to Australia."

The green eyes were unperturbed as she glanced at him. "This journey will not be quite as planned," she said, "this journey — " Then she stopped, turning the cup around and around in a puzzled way. Then she put it down on the tray, "I'm not in the mood for fortune-telling," she said, resuming her knitting with an air of finality.

Asta had never been superstitious, but a cold shiver went down her back. Mrs Murdoch was upset for some reason. The trained eyes of a nurse could see the cold dew on the woman's upper lip, the hands holding the knitting were shaking so much that she nearly dropped it.

The other passengers, being not so perceptive, clamoured to have their own fortune told, but Mrs Murdoch hunched her shoulders and almost seemed to disappear into them. Whatever she'd seen, thought she'd seen, or pretended she'd seen, it wasn't pleasant — that was obvious.

Vida was fast asleep, and Asta settled back, pretending to do the same. Soon after, her heart started to thump madly as Larry stood up, and coming over, leaned down where she and the sleeping child were. He picked up the teddy-bear which had fallen on to the floor of the plane and tucked it more securely under Vida's blanket.

Opening her eyes just enough to see what was happening, Asta hoped the heightened colour his move had brought to her cheeks wouldn't be noticed.

Reaching up to a rack over her head, Larry pulled out another blanket and softly tucked it around Asta's knees. She forced herself to keep quite still as Larry switched off the light over her seat, but her thoughts were tumultuous.

Would he have bothered to make such a gesture unless? No, don't be stupid. He'd promised Mr Crane to look after them both. He was doing just that. Tears forced themselves through her eyelids, whether of self-pity, or remorse, or just the torment of having Larry's hands touch her without being able to respond, Asta wasn't clear, but she blinked them away determinedly. She went up to the back seat, where the last two passengers, a Mr and Mrs Montgomery, were sitting. They were so wrapped up in each other they'd hardly had a word to say to anyone else.

She was a minute, glossy black-haired girl with enormous eyes that were magnified by the glasses she wore, making them seem like pools of night-shadowed water in her tiny wedge of a face. It wasn't until they had met in the luxuriously appointed ladies' room that Asta saw she was in an advanced state of pregnancy.

"We're going to Australia for the

first time," she told Asta, "I'd never even been out of Scotland before, it's a bit scarey. Jamie, that's my husband, is joining one of Mr. Crane's firms, as an engineer."

"Have you somewhere to live?" asked Asta. "I mean, with the baby coming. I've heard that houses are as difficult to get in Australia as they are in England."

"Oh yes!" The girl's voice, with its Scottish accent was eager. "Mr Crane had seen to all that. He's been terribly kind, and we've nothing to worry about on that score."

Her voice had a proud ring. "My Jamie's a very clever engineer." Then she looked at Asta a little unhappily. "Of course, I shall miss England, and all my friends."

"You'll soon make others," said Asta, confidently. The girl didn't look much more than eighteen, she thought, and her husband, a very tall boy with untidy fair hair and dark-lashed blue eyes, couldn't be more than a few years older. One couldn't help noticing his evident devotion and attention to his girl-wife.

"I'm working my passage," Asta told her, with a smile, "if you can call it working. I've hardly seen the little girl I'm supposed to be looking after. She's Mr Crane's daughter. She was at the hospital where I was, and seemed to take a fancy to me, so he offered me the trip."

"You're a nurse then?" Mrs Montgomery's voice sounded relieved and pleased at the news.

Asta warmed to the girl. After all, even in these modern days, it takes some pluck to travel to the other side of the world to have your first baby.

The husband had left his seat when they returned to the body of the plane, and Asta sat with his wife for a while. Then the girl explained why she was feeling nervous. "You see," she said, "we didn't want to upset Jamie's parents by telling them the baby was already on the way when we married.

165

They're very religious, and terribly old-fashioned, but I love them both. They insisted on a white wedding, and a huge reception. I think they wanted to make up to me for being an orphan. They're such dears I just couldn't let them be disappointed in me — or Jamie, either. This offer to come to Australia was a marvellous chance. It's only for three years, and we can come home again if we want. We can just pretend the baby's premature, can't we? I'm afraid even Mr Crane doesn't know how close the baby is to being born. He mightn't have offered me a seat on the plane if he had. You see? I wanted to travel with Jamie — I couldn't bear to be left behind. It's such a splendid opportunity for him, and he would have probably have turned it down if I hadn't been able to travel with him."

"I see," said Asta, encouragingly, "well, don't worry about a thing, Mrs Montgomery."

"Oh please call me Flora," said the

girl, "I'm so glad you're on the plane, Nurse — "

"Asta," she said, smiling, "Now let me make you comfortable on your bed. And try to relax. We should be safely in Sydney in a few hours. In any case, there's a doctor on board, isn't there? The tall redheaded man in the front; and I'm a fully trained nurse, so it could be worse, couldn't it? Plenty of babies have been born in taxis and ambulances under far worse conditions. Anyway, it may be weeks yet — unless?"

"It may be the excitement of travelling," the girl said, her voice trembling a little, "I've never been on a plane before, but I've had one or two twinges. I'm terrified it may happen before we get there."

"You just put yourself in my hands," said Asta, firmly. "My own little charge is no bother at all, and takes very little of my time. We'll let down your seat now, and you put your feet up and relax. It's probably a false alarm. First babies do like to make an entrance. Perhaps it might be a good idea to get you into a nightie and dressing gown."

Flora's look was pathetically grateful. "I was so afraid of telling Jamie," she said. "I feel better now that you know."

"Your husband can sit in my seat until I'm sure you're OK and off to sleep. I'll sleep beside you if it'll be a comfort."

Asta hadn't been asleep herself for more than an hour or two when she felt a gentle tug at her sleeve, and heard the frightened little gasps of the girl beside her. A few questions soon cleared up any doubts in Asta's mind. The sprig of the Montgomery clan was going to make an appearance somewhere in the near future.

Pressing the bell for the stewardess, Asta reassured Flora as quietly as possible. All the other passengers seemed to be asleep by now. Oggie, the Norwegian girl, who was on duty, came out yawning, but was wide awake at once as soon as Asta explained the situation. She was quite unperturbed at the news. "It won't be the first time I've had to help deliver a baby," she said. "There's a nice little cabin at the rear, kept for anyone who feels ill. There's a comfortable bed in there, and we'll be nice and quiet."

Asta gave a relieved sigh. "Thank goodness for that. Give Mrs Montgomery a hand out there, will you? I'll get my bag. I have most of the things we'll need in there. I don't want to wake Doctor Groves until it's necessary. It may still be hours yet. We may well get to Sydney before the baby comes. Would it be possible to let them know at the airport, do you think? They might have an ambulance waiting."

"I'll go up front and have a word with the pilot, Jack Daimler," said Oggie, "he'll know what to do."

Her tall, graceful figure disappeared through a door marked 'Private, Staff only. Strictly no admittance.' She hadn't been away for more than two minutes before she came running out, her face paper-white, lips pressed together with shock and fear.

Asta, standing at the door of the little cabin where the prospective mother had been made comfortable, closed it behind her, and met the stewardess outside.

She leaned over and hissed in Asta's ear, "The pilot," she said, "and Harry, too, the co-pilot, they're both terribly ill. Jack thinks it may be food poisoning from some lobster they had before leaving. They've been putting off calling for aid, because they thought they could stand it, but you should see them, Nurse. I don't know how they've managed to keep at the controls. Jack says we're on the automatic pilot at the moment. He's got double vision, he says, and can't even see the controls. Harry is the worst, he's passed right out on the floor. We must do something, quickly."

"You stay with Mrs Montgomery,"

she said. "I'll wake the doctor and see what we can do for them. I've given her a slight sedative, and she may sleep now. For heavens sake don't tell anyone else about this; we don't want a panic on our hands. Just smile, in case anyone isn't asleep. Tell Mr Montgomery his wife's all right, and to get some rest himself."

Making her way back to Larry's seat, she woke him, and quietly told him of the situation. She woke Ken, too, in case Vida should wake up and be frightened.

"Righto," said Ken, yawning, "if she wakes up, I'll sing her a lullaby."

Larry reached for his case. "I've got most things that might be of use," he said. "Come and help me, Asta."

The scene that met their eyes in the crowded cockpit of the plane was of sheer horror. Harry, the co-pilot, a middle-aged man with greying hair and a short dark beard, was lying on the floor, his body doubled up, knees under his chin, and a ghastly blue

171

tinge on his florid face. Jack Daimler was only fractionally better, obviously keeping conscious by sheer will power, but groaning with the effort. "Bloody fools," he gasped, "we've been warned not to eat anything like shell-fish before a trip. I did manage to bring some of it up into a bag, and I thought it might be over, but it keeps coming back, worse every time."

Larry's face was set and grim. "I want to give them a stomach wash-out," he said. "It's a bit late now; the stuff will have moved well down, but it's a chance. See what you can rouse up in the galley," he said to Asta. "A funnel; I have some rubber tubing in my bag, a bucket, large jug. Anything that'll be useful, you know the drill."

He was busy preparing an injection from his bag. "This'll ease the pain, I hope. For God's sake why didn't you call me earlier?"

"How's Harry?" asked Jack, his face contorted as another spasm went through him. "He had more than I did, and couldn't bring any of it up. I know I should have stopped at our last port of call, when we landed for fuel, but it seemed to have passed off for a while, and there's such a devil of a hoo-hah in these foreign places if they think you're ill. With the boss's kid on board, I couldn't risk it. Harry wasn't so bad then, either, and I thought we'd make it."

Even as Asta looked at him his face turned an ashen grey, and the pulse she felt for was thready, almost imperceptible. Larry was on the floor, attending to the other man, but his face was grave as he looked up at Asta. "I don't want to frighten you, Asta," he said, "but we've one hell of a problem on our hands. I don't know how long an automatic pilot works, or even *how* it works, but I don't think they're meant to take over landing, and so on. Unless I can pull the pilot out of this coma, we shall probably cruise around until the fuel gives out — and then — "

7

ANNIE, sleepy-eyed, and dressed in a short towelling bath-robe, her small feet thrust hastily into a pair of fluffy blue slippers, put her head round the door of the cockpit. She blinked, and gave her head a slight shake, unable to believe the scene in front of her. "What's happened to Jack?" she asked, then, her eyes coming into clearer focus, "and Harry, too? Are they ill? Why didn't Oggie waken me? She's overdue for her rest period, and anyway, she's supposed to call me if there's any trouble."

In a few words, Asta explained the situation, not trying to conceal the seriousness in any way. She knew at once that this small dark-eyed girl was well trained for her job. There was no trace of panic, just a slight setting of the delicate jawline.

Larry, going from one man to the other, said, angrily, "What I can't understand is why this plane is in the hands of two men only, with no stand-by for such an emergency. This sort of thing should be covered. Anything less is simply criminal. Even a lighthouse has to have a three-man crew. All the money that's been lavished on a plane like this, and they economise on man-power. Mr Crane's own daughter on it, too — it's simply God-damned crazy."

Annie, so calm until now, gave a gasp of utter dismay, her hand clutching the side of the door, and the blood draining from her face until it was clown-white. After the way she seemed to have accepted the danger of sudden death, it shook Asta to see her go to pieces now.

Then her voice, thin and trembling, cut into the disturbed atmosphere. "It's all my fault," she wailed, "all my fault. All because of my own stupidity."

"Pull yourself together," said Larry,

175

kneeling beside Harry, his voice irritated beyond measure. "This isn't the time for a show of histrionics. Pull yourself together, girl, and find something to do. The fault lies with the owners of the plane, in not providing proper cover."

"No!" Annie persisted, "There *should* have been another pilot on stand-by, there always has been. *Danny*. We're engaged to be married. At least, we were. I broke it off because I thought he'd been drinking too much. No one else noticed it. We hid it pretty well, or he'd have lost his job, but when I said we were through, just before we left London, he rushed off, probably on another drinking bout. I thought he'd be bound to catch us up at Orly, where we were due to pick up some more cargo. He's done that before — come in a friend's private plane, and no one was the wiser. I never thought he'd really miss the plane, never." She choked back the tears.

"I didn't really mean to break off

our engagement, only to teach Danny a lesson. When he didn't come aboard at Orly, I was a bit frightened, but not too much. I was terribly busy, and there's a pilot's rest room. He could have slipped in there when I wasn't looking, to sleep it off, especially if he'd been drinking. I was pretty sure he'd lie low just to punish me, or let me simmer down. I didn't want him to think I cared too much, so I left it."

"It was some time after we'd taken to the air again that I took in some coffee, in case Jack called for him, and then I realised he wasn't on the plane. I came and told Jack and Harry at once, in case they wanted to turn back, or anything, but Jack was furious. He said there was nothing to do but carry on without him. He said — he said — he'd see that Danny never worked on an airline again. Now I think of it, he must have been feeling a bit ill then. He was very pale, but he's got a terrible temper, and it would only have made things worse. I got them both some coffee, put it down by their side and rushed off again. I'd only have made things worse if I'd said anything about his looking ill. Jack is one of those men who'll never admit to as much as a headache.

"I went and told Oggie that Danny wasn't aboard, of course, but she didn't seem to think it mattered all that much. She agreed it was better to leave things until we arrived in Sydney. Jack would have cooled down by then and might be persuaded to give Danny another chance. I still think something must have happened to keep Danny. He loves his job, in spite of everything. If only I hadn't been so beastly to him, this would never have happened. I just went on with my work, praying things would turn out right, and Danny might have a really good excuse for not joining the plane."

She hesitated pathetically at the door, looking rather like a naughty little girl in her blue bathrobe and Larry grunted, "Sorry I flew off the handle, Annie, you couldn't possibly have foreseen anything like this. Go and get dressed, there's a good girl, and keep a good supply of coffee going."

"I've often heard them say that a third pilot wasn't really necessary," she said, "this plane is a proto-proto — "

"Prototype?" asked Larry. "I'd say it must be from the way we're hurtling through the air. It's certainly different from any plane I've ever travelled in so far. No wonder Mr Crane is so proud of it. He was telling me it looks after itself most of the time, on pre-set course, and that running it is a piece of cake. The trouble is that even a piece of cake has to be put together by someone who knows how to cook. The plane still needs someone to take off and land. Those rows of dials on the instrument panel might as well be a line of hieroglyphics as far as I'm concerned. Anything over the four on my car dashboard confuses me. A car would have an instruction book — that's more than we're likely to find here."

There was a steely look in Larry's eyes as he bent over Jack. "Unless we can get one of these men on his feet, or at the very least able to give some instructions, before we approach Australia, we're going to come down into the sea, or crash land on Sydney Harbour Bridge. Even if this plane does know its way home, it's going to need someone behind that horrifying collection of dials and controls."

Leaning over Harry, he lifted one lid, and peered into a glazed blue eye, then straightened his back wearily. "No sign of improvement yet. Are all the passengers asleep, Annie?" he asked the girl, who was still hovering by the doorway.

She peered into the semi-darkened body of the plane, and nodded silently. "They seem to be, Doctor. No one's moving."

"Is there such a thing as a folding chair, or anything we can carry the two men in? I want to get them into bed, with hot-water bottles if you have such things on the plane."

"Yes, we have," she said, eager to be doing something. "There's a folding stretcher too, in the locker room, with a lot of first-aid stuff."

"Get it," said Larry, tersely. "We've got to be very quiet about it. It should be possible to carry them down that gangway between the seats. It's wide enough. We don't want to frighten any of the others if we can help it."

Turning to Asta, as the stewardess crept quietly down between the sleeping passengers, he said, "I don't think we have much of a chance with Harry, not without proper treatment. I can't do any more than get him into a warm bed. His pulse is very faint, and I don't like the clamminess of his skin. If only they'd called me as soon as they felt ill. We've just got to get the other one functional — all our lives depend on it. Heavens, what a mess, Asta. Thank God you're not the hysterical type, but I'm a bit apprehensive of what the reaction of some of the passengers will

181

be if they get any inkling that this plane is shooting along, thousands of feet up, with no one at the controls."

One at a time, with the aid of the stretcher Annie brought up, they managed to get the two pilots into a small room at the end of the plane, undress them, and get them into the two bunk-beds. No one had been disturbed, except for little Vida, who had wakened, demanded a drink and that her teddy should once more be found and placed inside the blankets. She soon went off to sleep again, however.

Larry leaned over the wide-awake Ken, and told him what was happening. "There's nothing you can do for the moment, old man," Larry told him. "If any of the others wake up, just say that someone was taken ill, but that everything's under control."

Ken nodded. "Call me if there's anything," he said. "I wish to God I could fly a plane for you. Maybe the pilot will pull through yet, eh?"

"One of them isn't quite as bad as the other," said Larry, "We can only hope."

Jack Daimler's colour was just fractionally better than it had been, and his breathing slightly less laboured, but he was still a very sick man, and Larry knew how quickly a condition as serious as his could worsen.

Asta, who was wrapping Harry in blankets, gave a gasp, and peered into the comatose man's face fearfully. "Quick, Larry," she called, "I think this one's stopped breathing."

"Get him on to the floor," said Larry, heaving the man from his bed. They went through the resuscitation routine, kiss of life, depressing the sternum in a rhythmic manner, until, the perspiration streaming down his face, Larry looked up at Asta and shook his head despairingly. "He's gone," he said. "He appears to have had a massive heart attack. We'd better concentrate all our efforts on the other man. He's our last chance. He's *got* to pull through, but God knows whether we'll do it in time. I don't have the least idea how close we are to Australia, but I do know that Mr Crane was boasting how fast the plane is. In fact, he wouldn't tell any of us how long it would take to get to Sydney, said he wanted to surprise us all, maybe set a new record."

"I don't think even the stewardesses know that," said Asta, "Oggie was telling me it's using an entirely new fuel, revolutionary, in fact, but she didn't know a great deal about it. It seems to be still rather hush-hush, she says. Mr Crane did say it will do enormous distances without stopping for refuelling."

Just then, Oggie came into the cabin, sleeves rolled up and her blue uniform dress covered with a large bath towel. "You'll have to come and help me, Nurse," she said, "I can't manage by myself. Annie called me outside and told me what's happened, but Mrs Montgomery — she's pretty near the baby's birth, and she keeps calling for you. I can't quieten her, and I'm afraid her husband may hear her and get worried."

Larry looked up from his patient and nodded at Asta. "All right, you go. There's nothing you can do here now. I'll call you if I have to, but you see to the mother. I daren't take my eyes of Jack, so you'll have to go it alone. Good luck, Asta. I can't let this one slip through my fingers too."

He gave Asta a brotherly pat on the back. "You're being just marvellous," he said. "Anyone would think we were in the operating theatre at St Margaret's instead of in danger of imminent death. I shall never forget the way you've coped with the situation." He didn't need to say 'If we come out of this alive,' but it was there in his eyes.

"You're being pretty marvellous yourself," she said, softly. "But we have the advantage over the passengers, don't we, Larry? It's one thing to be too busy to think and quite another to just sit in your seat and wait for it to

185

happen. What I'm mainly concerned with is keeping it from them for as long as possible — I couldn't bear to have little Vida frightened by someone else's terror."

"No, you're right," he said. "They might behave well, but it only needs one of them to have a fit of hysterics to make the situation even more tense."

On an impulse, Asta leaned over and kissed Larry's cheek. "Let's be friends, Larry," she said. "There's no time now for pettiness, is there?"

Without waiting for his reaction or answer, she flew into the small cabin where they were waiting for her.

"The pains are coming every few minutes now," said Oggie, her fair skin flushed. "She's doing very well, I think. Everything seems to be normal, but I'm glad to see you here." Turning away from the girl on the bed, so that her face was hidden, she said "I've told Mrs Montgomery the doctor has an ill patient, but he'll be on call if we find it necessary."

Going over to the young mother, Asta forced a reassuring smile. "Everything's going to be fine," she said, trying to keep her voice light-hearted in spite of the dread in her heart.

Surely fate couldn't be so unkind as to bring this new life into the world to snuff it out within hours — or even minutes — of being born? You read of terrible things like famine, earthquakes, drought, and felt sorry for the people who suffered; thousands of children had died that way, and yet, when it was so close, it seemed impossible to believe.

All this because Annie had had a tiff with the standby pilot. Asta felt sorry for the girl. She must be feeling terrible about the whole thing.

Last night, too, when everyone had been preparing to go to sleep, she'd noticed the two women who sat together, Mrs Murdoch and Mrs Munt. They had crossed themselves, and handled their rosaries before settling down. Was it right to allow them to

187

meet their deaths so unprepared?

She wondered, a little idly, whether Mrs Murdoch had really seen something in the tea-leaves. What had she said? "This journey will not be as planned." Asta could still see the woman turning the cup round and round, then refusing to go on.

Although she had no belief in the supernatural, perhaps because she'd never encountered it, Asta couldn't prevent a little shiver, as though an icy finger had touched her spine. "Come on, silly," she murmured to herself. "If Mrs Murdoch was really any good at seeing into the future, she wouldn't be on the plane at all, would she?"

Sitting by Flora's bed, encouraging and reassuring her, Asta knew the baby was certainly very near its appearance. "What about hot water?" she asked Oggie, standing near. There must be a galley — go and see, will you?"

"Yes," Oggie brightened at having something positive to do. "Ah Soy. He's the Chinese cook. None of the

188

passengers ever see him. He's not very
nice to look at — he was in a fire and
is badly scarred. But he's a wonderful
chef, and has his own little cubby hole
behind the galley. I'll go and see him,
and get him to make coffee for us all,
too, shall I?"

"Good," said Asta. "Take some in
for Larry too, Doctor Groves, that is.
He has it black, with two spoonsful of
sugar."

If Oggie wondered about why Asta
should know the doctor's taste in coffee,
she gave no sign of this.

What years it seemed since Asta had
been in her mother's kitchen, with
Larry, screwdriver in hand, stopping for
a cup of coffee. So warm and safe.

The plane was so silent and smooth
it seemed almost a dream that they
were in the air at all. Asta stood
up and went over to the porthole.
Far beneath them, partly hidden by
tiny cotton-wool clouds, was the sea,
silvery under the moon, and stretching
as far as the eye could see. If the

plane went down over the ocean, she thought, there would be no chance of survival at all. They would just sink without trace. Even if there was any survival kit on board, they might be thousands of miles from land. There would, no doubt, be the means of sending out distress signals, but none of them would know how to use them.

What odd things come to mind. Dick's father would be in his element now, sending out Morse signals. It would take rather more than a whole troop of Scouts to get them out of this situation though.

If she had married Dick, she wouldn't have been here at all, but with some wonder even at herself, Asta knew she would rather be with Larry, even in this situation — or perhaps *especially* in this situation. The quick blood came to her face as she thought of Larry saying "I shall never forget the way you've coped with this." It wasn't a love speech — in fact it might have been given to any competent nurse, but she treasured the way he'd said it. At least she'd proved herself to be more than the empty-headed female he seemed to have thought her.

Annie, the other stewardess, seemed to have disappeared after getting dressed, and Asta felt a little guilty about her. Poor kid, she must be going through her own private hell just now. Wondering whether she was all right, Asta looked down the rows of seats outside. At the far end, Ken was sitting, with one arm round Annie, whose face was buried in his jacket. Ken, seeing Asta, put a finger to his mouth then gave the 'thumbs up' sign. Better leave her where she was. There was nothing she could do just then.

A sharp cry from the bed sent Asta hurrying back to her patient. Oggie had brought a plastic apron, printed with a design of pot herbs on a red background, together with a large roll of hand towelling, and Asta used them to protect the bed. The baby's head was already visible.

"One more good contraction," she told the heaving Flora, "and it'll all be over. Don't push yet — I'll tell you when. Breathe through your mouth, that's a good girl, you're doing fine. Now again. That's it. Again — "

Asta hadn't done a great deal of midwifery since finishing her training, but the things she had learned flashed through her mind now. Thank God there were no complications, everything straightforward and text-book clear. She realised with surprise and gratitude that the procedures she'd learned were coming as smoothly as though she'd been doing this every day.

She'd assisted at births before, but never alone, and always in sterile, prepared conditions with everything to hand, and all the responsibility on someone else's shoulders.

She could call Larry, but if she did it could just be at some crucial moment, when Jack's breathing might stop, as Harry's had, and a doctor must be on the spot.

No, she wouldn't call him. This must be her own contribution to the crisis. If Jack died while Larry wasn't there, she might have the lives of all these people on her hands.

There were a few moments of panic, when she longed for support. Then the moment of birth came and she held the wet, slippery little bundle in her hands. Within seconds the baby was bawling lustily, and Flora's eyes were full of questions.

"A beautiful, beautiful boy," she told the exhausted mother. "Let Oggie just clean him up a bit and you shall see him for yourself."

Wrapping the child in a clean towel, she handed him to Oggie, who had just set down a tray with cups of coffee and biscuits.

Oggie was overcome with wonderment. "Isn't he the most wonderful thing," she said, and then, before Asta could stop her "What a pity if — " She caught Asta's eye and stopped, embarrassed at her own stupidity, blushing at her own gaffe. It didn't escape the anxious young mother, either, who tried to sit up in bed with a look of fear in her enormous eyes.

"What did she mean, Asta? A pity if what? Is there something wrong with my baby? There *is* isn't there? Tell me Asta, I must know." She pushed back the blankets that Asta had tucked around her. "I'll get out and see for myself if you don't tell me."

Pushing her firmly back on the pillow, Asta said "Your little son is everything he should be, Flora. You have my word. I'll show you in a minute. All his fingers and toes and a voice like a foghorn. I expect Oggie was going to say it's a pity his father couldn't have seen him born. Lots of fathers do these days, don't they? Only there wouldn't have been room in here, would there?"

"Maybe I can persuade Ah Soy to lend us his kitchen scales," said Oggie, "I bet that baby is in the eight pound range."

"I'd like to see my husband," said Flora, satisfied with Asta's explanation at last. "I want him to see his son. Please, wake him if he's asleep, will you? I know he'd want you to."

Nodding to Oggie, she took the baby, wrapped in a blanket and put him on the bed by his mother's side.

The cabin was soon tidied, and Asta had just drunk her coffee when there was a tentative knock on the door, and Jamie Montgomery's tall thin figure appeared, his face wreathed in broad smiles.

He leaned over the bed and kissed his wife, then poked a finger to part the blanket so that he could see the baby's face.

"Gosh!" he said, overcome with emotion. "Gosh! A wee laddie. A bonny wee laddie."

"Don't take too much notice of Jamie," said his wife, with a mischievous little smile, "he's apt to lapse into Burn's dialect when he's moved."

Jamie sat down on a chair which

Asta put by the bed, and held his wife's hand. "I was terrified when I knew Flora might be going to have the baby right away," he told Asta. "When you think of all the things that can go wrong. I've been blaming myself all night for bringing her on to the plane so near her time. Job or no job, it wouldn't have been worth while if anything had happened to my Flora."

"It was my own fault, Jamie," she said, softly, "but it's all over now." Then she gave a merry little laugh that relieved all the tension. "I'm wondering, Jamie, which country we're going over just now? Will it affect little Jamie's nationality?"

While they were all laughing at the idea, Asta remembered something Flora had said early on. "My Jamie's a clever engineer."

There are all sorts of engineers, she knew — civil, structural, mining. There must be dozens of them. There was just the remotest chance that this young man might be something to do with planes. Aeronautical engineering was it? Maybe a man who designed planes wouldn't necessarily be able to fly one, but they had to grasp at any straw.

She would have to ask him, and give the reason for asking too, but how to do it without frightening Flora, still weak from giving birth?

The new young father broke into her thoughts with "Oh! Who's ill, by the way? I thought I'd find the doc with Flora. Not that you haven't done a wonderful job, Nurse, and we're both grateful. Is it serious? I caught a glimpse of the doctor through a half-open door of the pilot's cabin, opposite. He appeared to be working on someone, pretty strenuously, I thought. All the passengers are in their seats, I've been walking up and down the gangway for ages, worried about Flora, and no one was missing. Is it the other stewardess? If there's anything I can do, you've only to ask. I'm immensely in your debt." He gave his wife's hand a squeeze, and touched the baby's blanket momentarily.

Her mind in a chaotic state, Asta thought furiously. She must trust that this young man would be able to cope with the knowledge of what might happen to his wife and son, perhaps in a few minutes, perhaps in hours. If there was any chance he might know enough to land the plane — anywhere, so long as it was on dry land. Any situation would seem a thousand times better so long as the danger of falling suddenly from the skies was over.

Composing her features and managing a smile, she said "If you can bear to leave your brand new son for a few minutes, I'll take you up on that offer. I could do with a hand outside. Yes, the doctor *is*, well, busy. Nothing to worry about."

"Sure!" he said, and kissed his wife tenderly. "Isn't it time you got some sleep, young woman?"

Leading the way to the deserted cockpit, Asta closed the door on them both. The deserted place, with the debris of their efforts to get the two pilots on their feet told part of the tale, without explanation.

Jamie took in the situation with a glance of horror. The he took command of his feelings, and apart from a tiny nerve working at the corner of his generous mouth, there was no sign of fear.

"Both of them?" he asked. "That must have been one of the pilots I saw the doctor working on, wasn't it? Is he — or should it be they — very bad? An accident, I take it?"

Asta gulped. "One of them is dead. The doctor suspects some virulent kind of food poisoning. He's working on the other one now, but he's still unconscious. The plane works on an automatic pilot — but it still has to be brought down. There should have been another stand-by pilot, but he didn't come on board. Can you do anything to help?"

Running long, slim fingers through

his unruly hair, Jamie said "I'm a mechanical engineer, I know nothing about flying a thing like this. Are you sure there's no one on board who could help? What about the other passengers? That fellow with the nice voice? Lots of young men take up flying these days, even someone with experience of small planes might have some inkling of how to get us down."

Then he snapped his fingers with a loud click. "I know!" There was an excited gleam in his grey eyes. "That awful bore, Sammy, as he insists on calling himself, was telling everyone how he'd been a bomber pilot during the war. His stories might be a product of his own imagination, but there's a chance, isn't there? I'll wake him and get him up here."

"Be careful how you do it," said Asta, "I don't want little Vida wakened before she needs to be. We shall have to tell the rest of the passengers sooner or later, but not while there's still a chance that Larry — the doctor — may pull the pilot out of his coma and get him well enough to at least direct operations. If that happens, we're all right, but we must prepare for the worst, mustn't we? We have enough to do without having to cope with hysterics. When you've got Mr Salmon up here, go and look after your wife, but not a word to her yet. She should be asleep; it would be natural for her to sleep now that the baby's here. At least we can keep it from her until the last moment, until — "

"Until we have to tell her that all her months of waiting, all our dreams of a new life together were in vain," he said, bitterly. "I'll get the man up here to you. If there's any truth in his tales at all, he must at least have some idea of how to land the plane with the least danger to us all."

Then he turned, and gave Asta an impulsive hug. "I always knew nurses were wonderful," he said, "but I didn't know how marvellous they could be.

Aren't you afraid for yourself? You must be."

"I'm terrified," admitted Asta, "but running up and down saying so wouldn't be much help, would it? A nurse's training at least *helps*. Annie and Oggie are pretty marvellous, too, you know. Annie is more upset on behalf of someone else on the plane — she feels she's to blame for the extra pilot not being on board, you know."

"And is she?" Jamie stopped at the door.

Asta shrugged. "How can anyone tell what our simplest actions may cause?" she said. "We'd never dare to do anything if we could know what repercussions there might be. Of course she's not to blame. How could she be? Stop at Ken's seat — he's the singer — and he knows what's happening. Tell him to keep an eye on Vida, and be ready to get her off the plane at once if we do manage a landing."

"Will do," said Jamie.

8

BOARDING the plane at the start of the trip, Larry hadn't been able to suppress a start of surprise at seeing Asta there. He'd assumed that little Vida's escort might be someone he knew, as a nurse from St Margaret's, but had never dreamed it might be Asta.

He realised now that she worked for an agency, and might be sent anywhere on a case. Then he knew he wasn't merely surprised at seeing her sitting there, tending her little charge, making her comfortable, and arranging a small family of dolls and animals around her.

Almost against his will there was a feeling of pleasure and relief, in spite of all his resolutions about women. For the first time, he had to admit he hadn't wanted to leave England and never see Asta again; that it mattered very much to know she would be near him for the duration of the journey. More, since he'd already assured Mr Crane he'd be calling as soon as Vida was home to give the child a check-up and make sure the trip had done her no harm.

Asta's mother had said before he left 'I wish you and Asta had been better friends, Larry, dear. You've been so kind to me. Perhaps you'll be coming to England again? You must promise to come and see us, Jim and I will be so happy to put you up.'

And he'd promised. Maybe if he stayed in Sydney for a year or so, that mysterious web Asta was throwing around him would disappear. He'd probably find Asta married, if not to Dick, then someone else, and although he told himself, over and over that if she *did* marry it would matter nothing to him, he knew it would. Matter a hell of a lot. Better keep away altogether.

What an abysmal fool he was, after

all that had happened to his brother. And Ken.

He'd been more than a bit stupid, he thought, angry with himself. There could be no mistaking that warm response when he'd kissed Asta — even if you allowed for the champagne. Maybe he should have followed it up, as nine out of ten men would have done, had an affair with her and got it out of his system. Yet, deep down, Larry knew it wouldn't have worked. It wouldn't have been enough to own Asta for a few days, weeks, or months. He longed for her to be there all the time, sharing his life.

He'd had affairs before, light-hearted ones that had hurt no one. One that had very nearly led to marriage, until that day when Alan had died brokenhearted.

With a feeling of contempt for his own weakness he remembered his remarks to Ken. "No girl's worth upsetting your life for. I haven't met the female who's even remotely likely to get me off my set course. If I so much as saw one looming on the horizon, I'd pack my bags and be off out of temptation." He'd been that confident. Then Ken's reply, "No one's immune, Larry. When you do fall, it may be harder than you think."

Well, he had packed his bags, hadn't he? Yet here she was, on the same plane, and if he wasn't careful, all that carefully erected façade he'd built was going to crumble, and he'd be putty in the hands of a girl who took pleasure in kneading a man's heart, pummelling it into a shapeless mass, then discarding it as useless.

Not, he thought, with a swift glance in her direction that Asta looked at all the part of a heartless siren, seeing the way she attended little Vida, and the child's obvious liking for her. Still, there must be that fatal flaw in Asta's character, taking pleasure in leading a man on. What did she really want from life, he wondered? She must like her work, not like some nurses who go into it as a means of earning a living until they can find a husband.

A girl with Asta's looks might have married any one of a number of doctors at St Margaret's. It hadn't escaped his notice how they all followed her with their eyes, the little mob at the hospital dances, all trying to get her to dance with them.

She could hardly have known he would be on the plane, Larry thought, bitterly; Asta had made it abundantly clear that she didn't welcome his company. Still, his broad shoulders squared themselves and his mouth firmed, this job was probably well paid, and it was comparatively simple, compared with some of the consignments she must have had at times; she merely had to keep an eye on a nice little kid until they arrived in Australia. Asta must have jumped at the chance — what girl wouldn't?

That enormously ostentatious bunch of red roses had really made him think. She must be keeping the poor devil on a string, to have sent them. Just playing with him, showing what power she had. How heavily scented the confounded things had been, quite overpowering. Give him the kind of girl who'd be thrilled with a bunch of violets, or primroses, any time. Not that Asta had received the gift with any show of enthusiasm, it was true. It hadn't escaped his notice how her face had clouded over when she read the card that came with them. What had she expected — a diamond bracelet tucked inside?

She'd looked almost angry when she thrust the flowers down by her seat. It appeared that someone had wasted an awful lot of money, after all.

It was much too late to do anything about the situation now, anyway. He'd given his assurance to Mr Crane that he'd look after both Vida and her nurse, and he intended to do just that, come Hell or high water.

A peculiar man, Andrew Crane. Self-made and extremely proud of the fact.

A tough man of business, yet Larry knew him as a philanthropist who had donated large sums of money to charity and was good to his employees. He had, in fact, helped Larry to stay at medical college when his father had died suddenly, leaving a lot of debts. He'd never asked anything in return, and wouldn't even listen to thanks.

Larry had been pleased to be asked to travel with Mr Crane's little daughter — he knew what she meant to him. It wasn't going to be much of a job, anyway, he'd thought. Vida was friends with everyone on the plane within minutes of take-off.

Mr Crane was being 'angel' to the new season of opera, too, and it gave Larry a glow of satisfaction to know that Ken was to have another chance to make good. He knew how much it meant to his old friend. Certainly Mrs Milne's little drama group had done the trick, Ken's inhibitions seemed to have melted. It only remained to see whether it would last on the big stage of the Opera House. The seat on Mr Crane's plane had been another gift — Ken just had to make good this time.

The only thing that disturbed Larry was having Asta sitting so close to him. He'd thought it would be easy to forget her, once he'd left England for good. He'd *wanted* to leave, wanted to erase her memory entirely from his mind. Get himself immersed in a new, exacting job, perhaps right away from civilisation, in the Bush. Perhaps he never would quite erase the memory of holding Asta in his arms, he'd thought, but in time it wouldn't hurt any more. Not so much, anyway.

And yet, once he'd glimpsed her there, with the sun shining through the porthole on to her hair, her face slightly flushed — those magnificently blue eyes shining — there was a perilous lurch in the region of his heart. He didn't flatter himself that the bright eyes and flushed cheeks were anything to do with seeing him. The excitement of the trip, probably, or maybe that fellow, Dick, seeing her off at the airport. Probably she'd promised him to return and carry on where they had left off.

"All right," he muttered to himself, giving a resigned shrug. "I'll be polite, pleasant, helpful. No point in being boorish. If anyone could be boorish to a girl who greeted you with such a sweet smile. Probably she'd made up her own mind to act in much the same way."

Even Ken had been struck with Asta's beauty after meeting her. "Now there's a girl," he'd said, with a low whistle. "A nurse, is she? You could almost set her to music, couldn't you? I notice you can't keep your own eyes off her, old chap. They're not *all* tarred with the same brush, you know, even if old Verdi did say 'Wayward is Womankind'. He wrote some super love songs too, you know. I could fall for Asta myself, but well — you two seem made for each other, Larry. Don't they say the best wife for a doctor is a nurse? And what a nurse, into the bargain! How's it going, Larry? Is she favourably inclined? You're a good-looking bloke, it shouldn't be difficult."

Larry gave him a wry look. "Asta, and me? So far she's slapped me down on every possible occasion. Anyway, I've no intention of falling in love with anyone, Ken. Maybe one day I'll pick some nice homely Australian girl and raise a little family of bush-whackers. When I think of Ian — it puts me off women, especially the good-looking kind."

"Good looks don't have to go with an empty head," said Ken. "And if you ask me, it's high time you settled down."

"I'm thirty-two next month," said Larry, "I'm used to being a bachelor now."

Ken's expressive eyes had twinkled a little, and he gave a disbelieving grunt. "Don't protest too much, old chap, I felt like that myself after that affair with Stella, but I'm beginning to think I could be wrong. I suppose it was a lucky escape, really. I might have married the girl. I don't think she liked music, come to think back — and I'd probably have given it all up just for a quiet life. There's no need for you to forego a happy married life if you meet the right girl, is there? I've always heard them say a doctor ought to be married — his female patients have more confidence in him, I suppose!"

Then Larry's thoughts came back to the present. To the ever-closer threat of the plane's crashing with little hope of any of them surviving.

His hand went up unconsciously to the spot where Asta's lips had touched it in a friendly gesture. In other circumstances his reaction would have been to take her in his arms again.

He bit his lips in an agony of realisation — that Asta was everything he'd ever dreamed of in a woman. Her

213

eyes, so gentle and solicitous when she bent over a patient. That trim little figure, deliciously curved, those hands that might have been on a Botticelli Venus.

Was he falling in love *now*, when every thought must be for the fate of all these people? Falling in love at just about the most bizarre and inopportune time? The strain must be going to his head, he thought, agonised at the responsibility of it all.

That terrible scene in the cockpit had come back with renewed force. The fight to revive the pilots — Asta had been wonderful, with no thought for her own safety at all. The way she'd coped with the young mother and her baby, too.

Larry had a look at his remaining patient, where Oggie sat watching every laboured breath. "All right, Oggie," he said, gently, "see if you can rustle up some more coffee, and then try to rest. It's not going to happen for a while, I'm pretty sure."

Examining Jack Daimler, Larry knew that if he pulled through at all it would be hours before they could get him out of bed. He was still in a semiconscious state, with a nasty blue tinge round his mouth. Everything that could be done had been done. They could only keep him warm see that he didn't suddenly stop breathing, and wait.

Larry cursed his total ignorance of the first rules of flying a plane. So many of his friends in Australia flew their own aircraft, but he'd never found the time to learn.

Then had come that first gleam of hope, with young Montgomery's suggestion. If Sammy had been a bomber pilot, he must a least have some idea of how to get them down to earth.

He must have been sitting there for hours when he woke up again, to find a cold cup of coffee by his side. It had been the sleep of utter exhaustion, he knew, but he was furious with himself. Jack could have died while he was sleeping there. His condition had hardly changed, however, still no sign of coming out of it, but perhaps a slight improvement in his breathing, a tinge more colour in his cheeks.

Had he been dreaming, or had someone said Sammy was a bomber pilot during the war? He jumped to his feet, feeling a heavy sense of guilt at the time he'd wasted.

He looked in at the room where the young mother was peacefully sleeping, and the two girls, Asta and Oggie were dozing in canvas chairs.

"Keep an eye on Jack, will you, Oggie?" he asked, "I've given him an injection, and he looks slightly better. Call me at once if there's any sign of his coming round, won't you?" He yawned wearily. "I've just had a look outside, the dawn's coming up, and we're passing over a large land mass. I have an idea it is New Zealand, but I can't be sure. We're too high up, and there's a lot of cloud about. I have to go and wake one of the passengers.

There's just a hope he might be able to get us down."

"Who?" asked Asta, curiously.

"The man who calls himself Sammy," said Larry. "He's about the last person I'd have thought possible, but now's his big chance. If he can do it, I'll take back all the uncharitable thoughts I had about him. I'm off to wake him up now. I hope I can do it without scaring the others."

"If Sammy can do it," said Oggie, with the ghost of a smile, "he'll be the hero of the century. He'll simply love it, won't he?"

"If he can bring us down to earth alive," said Larry, fervently, "I'll take back every unkind thought I had about him."

"Ah Soy, the chef, is about," said Oggie, "he never sleeps for long, and I think he's getting a bit suspicious about things. Should we tell him do you think, Doctor? I can't imagine him getting into a state. He's quite imperturbable."

"Not just yet," said Larry. "Ask him to get on with preparing breakfast will you? It'll help to keep everyone from wondering if we keep to the normal schedule. Try to eat something, you girls, and good luck. I'm off to waken Sammy." He turned at the door and looked back at them admiringly, "I don't know who had the better training for this kind of situation," he said, "but both kinds seem to work. You're marvellous, both of you."

Oggie smiled her thanks, then rose and went to the other cabin, where Jack was, while Larry went quietly down the aisle to where the red-faced Sammy was snoring gently.

Shaking him gently by the shoulders, Larry leant over and whispered into one crumpled red ear "Wake up, Mr Salmon. Wake up, there's a good chap. We need your help urgently."

With a loud and final snort Sammy woke, stretching his arms in a luxuriant yawn that showed his discoloured teeth, coated with nicotine.

"Wassa marrer?" he enquired, testily. "Disturbing a chap's beauty sleep. I don't have early morning tea. Take it away."

"Please," said Larry, in a stage whisper, "don't awaken the others. I must talk to you, it's very urgent or I wouldn't have disturbed you. I want to talk to you outside. Please follow me."

Sammy closed his eyes again, firmly. "What the Devil do you want me for, at this ungodly hour?" he complained. "If you want anything done, ask old Homer here. He's a great DIY man. I want at least another hour's sleep before I get up. This is supposed to be a private plane, isn't it? I thought I was going to have a nice rest after my year's work."

Mr Homer Pidgeon's dark face broke into a wide smile. "If there's anything I can do," he said. "I know there's something gone wrong. I'm a light sleeper, and I saw them carry out the pilots."

"Thank you, Mr Pidgeon," said Larry, "but not unless you can — " He stopped, afraid to break the news to Sammy too quickly, and risk a loud outburst so near the other sleeping passengers.

Homer nodded understandingly. "No, doctor, I can't do that, I'm sorry to say. Drop us a few hundred miles away from home, and I'll lead you back, even if I have to feed you on wichetty grubs." He smiled again, showing a perfect set of large white teeth.

Larry looked hastily at Sammy, but he was still half asleep, and didn't appear to have taken in the conversation. "Thanks," said Larry, "just keep an eye on things, will you, Mr Pidgeon. If there's anything you can help with, I'll call on you." He shook the slumberous Sammy once more, roughly this time with an urgency that at last got through.

"Quietly, please. Follow me, I must talk to you." He helped the still sleepily yawning Sammy into a flamboyant

Japanese dressing-gown, with gold dragons embroidered on the back and sleeves. Sammy at last came to full realisation that something was really amiss, and lumbered after Larry into the cockpit of the plane.

He quickly closed the door on them, but not before Sammy had let out a yell. "Bloody Hell!" The man's slack jaw, with its dark stubble of beard, fell dramatically, and his tiny eyes protruded even more than usual, as he took a disbelieving look around the disordered cockpit.

"Where's the pilot?" he demanded. "What's going on here? I shall have something to say to Mr Crane when I see him. I'll tell you that for nothing. Someone should be at those controls, shouldn't they? Been drinking have they?" He gave a disgusted look at the materials they'd used for pumping out the pilots' stomachs.

"The plane is flying on automatic pilot," said Larry, ignoring the man's remarks. "Both the pilots have been taken ill with what I imagine to be food poisoning. Lobster, to be exact. In fact, one of them is dead, and the other in very bad shape."

"Oh! Sorry, Doc. But it's not as bad as that, is it? I mean, there has to be another pilot on board. Mr Crane introduced me to him. Danny something or other. Seemed a nice chap. I had a couple of drinks with him at the airport. Bit under the influence, I thought, but he's had plenty of time to sleep it off now, eh! Curled up, somewhere, that's where Danny is. Someone told me he goes on the occasional binge."

He yawned again, and stretched his arms hugely. "Qualified pilot, and all that, though. No need to have woken me up, you see? Didn't the girls tell you about him? Covering up, I shouldn't be surprised. Some of you people, making mountains out of — well, I mean, I'm sorry about the pilot, of course, Doc. Which one was it died?"

"It was Harry, and it's no molehill.

Danny didn't join the plane at all. He was left behind. Annie didn't report him missing because she hoped he'd catch the plane up at Orly. She didn't even know he *hadn't* until it was too late, and we were on our way. The other pilots should have turned back I suppose, but they didn't. No one could have foreseen both of them being struck down like that, could they?"

"Someone should have been responsible for seeing we had a full crew," said Sammy, furiously. "Those stewardesses — they must have known — I'll have something to say to them."

"The girls have been wonderful," said Larry. "They've known the danger we're in for hours now, and not a whimper from them. You'll kindly leave them alone. The other passengers, too. They're not to be told until we have to. Unless we can get someone to land us, somewhere, anywhere, we shall just go on flying around until the fuel gives out and we drop. I did manage to locate the fuel gauge, and it shows about a quarter full. I've no idea how long that will last, though. I brought you out here because I understand you were a bomber pilot during the war, Mr Salmon. You must know more about it than any of us."

"Me?" The man's ruddy face drained to a putty colour. "All those stories I tell are just to keep people amused. I wouldn't have a clue. I was ground-staff in the RAF. You know how it is with a salesman, you have to have a nice lot of tales to tell. Nobody expects 'em to be true."

He clutched at Larry's arm convulsively, "You've got to get the other pilot out here. He can't be so bad you can't strap him to his seat, or something, man. He should be able to land this thing with his eyes shut."

"That's precisely what they are at the moment," said Larry, grimly, "Shut. Tight shut. He's had an injection. There's no hope of his coming round for some hours."

Sinking into one of the pilots' seats, Sammy put his head in his hands and howled. "How can you just stand there so calmly, Doctor? We're all going to die."

His voice became a squeal, like that of an animal seeing the knife. "I've got everything to live for. I've just had the best sales year ever. Mr Crane thinks a lot of me. He says so."

"Mr Crane thinks a lot more of his little daughter," sad Larry, sickened by the man's attitude. "There's a newly born baby on the plane, too, did you know that? Those three brave girls — don't you think I'd do anything to save their lives? All we can hope for now is that the pilot will recover enough before we run out of fuel. Come on man, pull yourself together. I don't want you to frighten the others. Breakfast will be served as usual. I suggest you go back to your seat, get your clothes, then wash and shave in the rest room. Try to look as normal as usual, and say nothing."

Sammy collapsed in his seat, every line of him a defeated warrior, his hands shaking, and his eyes glazed with fear.

"I can't, Doc," he whispered, "I just can't. My legs won't hold me. I feel sick. You must do something for me. I'm not one of your flaming heroes, just a salesman. It's all right for you. You deal with death all the time. I don't even like seeing anyone ill, or hurt."

Larry's first reaction was to take the man by the shoulders and shake him, angrily, but he could see the terror in those little black eyes, the convulsive shaking of his limbs. If he allowed the fellow to return to the main body of the plane like this, it would be obvious to anyone who saw him that something was seriously wrong.

It was a terrible blow, too. He had pinned his hopes on Sammy being capable of at least getting them all down in one piece.

Putting his head round the door, he beckoned to the Aborigine, Homer Pidgeon, even in this atmosphere suddenly realising what a strange name it was. Suitable for one of those top stars, he mused; they always appeared to be looking for strange and unusual names for themselves. Still, it was reasonable enough. Starting off in life with a name like Pidgeon, he supposed, the Homer part must have come naturally. He put his fingers to his lips, but there was no need; the dark-skinned man crept stealthily up to him, liquid eyes full of questions.

"Could you go quietly to the pilot's cabin, at the other end of the plane," he asked, "and ask the stewardess or the nurse to give you my bag."

Swiftly Larry prepared an injection and, rolling up the sleeve of the unprotesting Sammy's dressing-gown, slid the needle into his arm.

"Help him back to his seat, will you?" he said. "He'll be out like a light in a few moments. Tuck him up, and if anyone asks, tell them he's had toothache, and I've given him a sleeping pill."

Homer nodded, and taking Sammy's

arm in his own strong one, half carried him back to his seat, where he collapsed like a tired baby who's been fed and changed.

Larry could see that Annie, whose colour had come back, had gone off to sleep with Ken's arm still around her.

"How is it?" Ken whispered. "Any news?"

Larry shook his head. "I thought we were on to something, but we're back where we started, Ken."

"The pilot? How is he?"

"Not much better, I'm afraid, but he's holding his own now. Thanks for looking after Annie. Poor kid. She feels badly about failing to report Danny not being on the plane."

"Damned shame," said Ken, softly, looking down at the flushed face in the crook of his arm. "She's a super kid, Larry. I persuaded her to take a good swig from my flask of brandy, and it did the trick."

"Best thing you could have done," said Larry. "She badly needed to relax.

Don't disturb her until breakfast comes round."

'Back where we started,' had he said? Not quite. They were so many miles nearer death, so many more gallons of fuel less than they had a few hours before. So much nearer the time when he must tell the passengers, including Mrs Montgomery, happy in the birth of her son, and the two women with their knitting. Somewhere at the back of his mind he could see another knitter — *The Tale of Two Cities*, wasn't it? Only the woman in that story was knitting away others' lives, not her own.

He wondered about the Chinese cook, whom no one but the stewardesses had seen. Would he want to meet his Gods suddenly, without preparation? It was such a terrible responsibility, keeping their impending doom from the people who didn't already know. Perhaps he would talk to Asta, ask her advice.

She was sitting quietly by the unconscious pilot's bedside, taking his pulse. Her face was white with tiredness and strain, and his heart leapt at seeing her.

How different she was from the girl he'd imagined her to be. How could he have had the nerve to label her as unreliable? His mind went back to that morning, when he'd been such an idiot over that American with the car. He must have seemed a condescending fool, to Asta. Then, when she'd shown some sign of being friendly, he'd treated her like a naughty child. Yes, he'd a lot to learn about women. Especially about this one. If only they came out of this alive, he wanted to spend the rest of his life studying her, loving her, doing everything for her. If they came out of it. If —

9

THE two stewardesses had finished serving breakfast and were sipping cups of tea in the kitchen.

"Poor Mr Montgomery looks a bit wan," said Annie. "It's terrible for him, seeing his wife so happy with the baby, and knowing what's going on."

"Yes," answered Oggie. "It must be pretty ghastly for him, poor man, his wife is absolutely bubbling over with plans for the future. He's sitting with her now, trying to look pleased about the baby, and knowing full well the poor little thing may have no future at all."

"I'll take him some coffee," said Annie, "He refused any breakfast. I heard him tell his wife he'd had his. She's tucking in to a big plate of devilled kidneys, and chattering away between mouthfuls."

Jamie Montgomery, sitting by his wife's bed, kept telling himself he ought to tell Flora, yet, tough little Scotswoman though she was, he was afraid. How could he bring himself to shatter the happiness she was feeling by telling her their lives were in danger?

Flora, giving her husband a puzzled look said "You don't look well, darling. Is everything all right? Worried about the new job? I'm sure you needn't be, Mr Crane wouldn't have offered it to you unless he had real confidence."

"I didn't sleep very well," he answered. "Worried about you, I expect."

She smiled at him, radiantly. "It's all over now, Jamie. We have our lovely little son. He's been fed and bathed. Nurse weighed him. Eight pounds and two ounces," she laughed. "A real monster. He looks just like you, Jamie. Even to the untidy quiff of hair over his eyes. I keep wetting my finger and trying to straighten it out, but it's hopeless. Have you eaten your breakfast? You don't look at all like a proud father. I'm a bit disappointed in you, darling. I thought you'd be as happy as I am."

Jamie forced a smile, and took a look at the child, rosy and contented in a make-shift cot they had made from a large cardboard packing case lined with blankets.

He touched the fair fuzz of hair on his son's head with a gentle forefinger, and had to turn away to hide the emotion that welled up inside. God! What a fool he'd been to risk bringing Flora here so near her time. They'd been so happy in Scotland. Plenty of couples had a seven-month baby. His parents would have been far too proud of their first grandson to have bothered. Squaring his shoulders, he turned back to his wife.

"I had some breakfast earlier," he lied. "I'll just watch you eat."

"Marvellous food," said Flora, hungrily, "we have a wonderful cook on board, don't we? A Chinese, Asta told me. Wouldn't you like some of these kidneys, darling? They're out of this world. I wonder where Mr Crane found him? The cook, I mean. You'd hardly think there's enough scope for a super chef on such a small plane, would you? He should be in a big hotel, or a liner."

"I don't think many people would employ him, poor devil," said Jamie. "I did catch a glimpse of him. He's terrible to look at. Scars I imagine even a plastic surgeon could do no more for. A lot of people wouldn't want to work with someone like that. He keeps entirely to the kitchen and his own quarters, I'm told. Only the two stewardesses see him during the trip. I went out to the kitchen for a drink during the night, not wanting to bother the girls, and he was out there. He turned away like a flash, and was gone, but not before I'd seen his face. Or what had been his face before the fire."

"Fire?" asked Flora, "was that how it

happened? How? Did they tell you?"

"Shot down in flames," said Jamie, "Annie told me, some Chinese border fight or other. This job must be a godsend to him. Another of Mr Crane's good deeds."

Then a look of realisation came over his face, and the china on his wife's breakfast tray rattled as he shot to his feet. "Pilot, pilot," he said, the words forcing themselves from his white lips, making Flora give him a startled look.

"Really, Jamie," she said, crossly, "you'll have to learn to move a bit more quietly you know. You'll wake the baby. What on earth's come over you now?"

"Sorry, my darling," he said, "Enjoy your breakfast. I've just remembered a message I should have delivered. I won't be long, I promise you."

"You'd better have a shave while you're out there, too. You'll scrape the baby's skin if you try to kiss him."

"I suppose I do look pretty terrible," he said, fingering the dark stubble on his chin. "Having a baby does put you out of your stride. I'll make myself presentable before I come back." Somehow he must keep up the pretence that all was well, but just now he had to see the doctor, and tell him what was burning into his brain. Kissing his wife's lips, a little buttery from the toast, he dashed out of the cabin, leaving Flora mystified but altogether too happy and contented with her lot to worry too much about her husband's strange behaviour.

Rushing into the cabin where Larry was attending to his patient, Jamie caught his sleeve. An old childhood stutter came back, and he was practically incoherent.

"What is it, Mr Montgomery? Your wife?" Then, more anxiously, "She's not haemorrhaging — No? The baby then? Sit down and get your breath, there's a good chap."

"Ah Soy," he managed to gasp out at last. "You know, Doctor, the Chinese cook. Did you know he was shot down from a plane? That's why he's so badly scarred. Mr Crane did tell me about him, but I was too worried about Flora to take much notice. I don't think even the girls have realised; he was a pilot! I'm pretty sure Mr Crane said he was flying the plane when it happened. You must talk to him Doctor. Tell him you're a medical man — he's very shy of seeing anyone. Why didn't I think of it before? He's just got to try, however remote the possibility of his being able to help."

Larry slapped the other's shoulder. "Good man. I'll go and interview this — Ah Soy is his name? No time to waste, is there? Can you sit here and keep an eye on Jack? He's a bit better, but any sign of choking, or of coming round, call Asta, she'll be able to cope. Your wife's OK?"

Jamie nodded, dumbly. "Flora's so happy it hurts to see her. I can't bear to watch. She'll be all right eating her breakfast. She was even talking some rubbish about walking off the plane at the airport. Says she never felt better in her life."

"Good." Larry nodded approvingly. Strolling in as leisurely a way as he could to the kitchen door, he pushed it open and entered. A large notice said 'Private. Strictly no admittance.' Larry wasted no time, but strode purposely into what was every woman's dream of a kitchen.

It smelt of the recently cooked breakfast, but already all the dishes had been washed and neatly stacked away in cupboards. Arranged along the walls were gleaming copper saucepans, kettles, moulds, griddles, and other utensils that could only be named by a dedicated cook.

One side of the long narrow room was taken up by a series of ovens, hot-plates, micro-wave cookers, toasters, coffee-pots, all polished to such a degree they reflected each other like a hall of mirrors.

The opposite wall held deep-freeze cabinets, fridges, cupboards, and a double-sided, stainless-steel sink with long-armed taps.

Larry could see a door at the other end, and as nobody answered his call, he walked through, once more disregarding the 'Private' notice on the polished mahogany, and stepped into a remarkable room.

Certainly it didn't belong to the world of planes, he thought, sniffing the heavy scent of the place. Was it incense? Or something more sinister? You half expected to be greeted by a beautiful girl with Oriental eyes and clothes.

He could see little for a minute in the subdued light coming from a decorated brass lamp hanging from the ceiling, but had the prickly sense of being watched.

Another small light with a red silk shade stood in front of what appeared to be the life-size figure of a woman. She had outstretched hands with jewelled rings on the slender fingers, but they looked menacing rather than extended in blessing. Her eyes, almost alive, shone green in the lamplight, with a slightly mocking glint in them. It was almost as though they were following his moves, Larry thought. Tearing himself away from the mesmerising glare of the statue, idol, or whatever it was, Larry saw the figure of a small man kneeling on the floor beneath the hands.

"I'm sorry to disturb you," he said, "but I must talk to you at once, please." Still the man kept his face turned away, though Larry's trained surgeon's eye noticed the small rosettes of red flesh where the ears should have been. The man wasn't deaf, however, for he said in a cultured voice "Will you please see one of the stewardesses if you have any complaints about the food. I do not interview, Sir."

"I am a surgeon," said Larry, quietly, "You need have no fear of me. It is nothing to do with the food, which is excellent. This is an extreme emergency, and you may be able to help. Please let me explain."

A slight hunching of the man's thin shoulder blades was the only reply. "It is no concern of mine," was the answer. "I cook the meals, nothing more. Please leave my quarters."

Larry's temper blazed at last. The strain of the past hours was beginning to creep up on him.

"Damn it man," he shouted, "this is a matter of life or death, for us all, as well as you!"

Once more the shoulders hunched. "Death? What is that to me? I know there is something wrong, the girls are strung up, nervous, that I already know. The plane has been in trouble for some time. We should have landed at Sydney Airport by now. Mr Crane confides things to me — he knows I never talk to anyone. Is it the new fuel? He was so confident about it."

"Confident enough to entrust his little daughter to the plane," said Larry. "Did you know she is on board? If you owe anything to Mr Crane, won't you at least try to save her? I have been told you are a pilot, Ah Soy. Is it true? Both the pilots were taken ill after we left. One of them has died, and the other is gravely ill and may not come out of his coma until it is too late. The stand-by pilot never showed at all, so we are on automatic."

At last the man got to his feet and faced Larry, who, used as he was to disfigurement, had to control his immediate reactions of pity and horror. Two black eyes peered from lids that had been grafted on by the surgeon's skill. Slabs of skin on the bones of his face were of varying hues, depending on which part of the body they had been taken from.

"I was fortunate, Doctor, as you see, they managed to save my eyesight." The slit where his lips should have been turned up in a wry grimace. "Not a pretty sight, eh? The two girls see very little of me, fortunately for them. I only have to slide the trays through the hatch. It's true I was a pilot. Doctor Groves, isn't it? I have a passenger list on the wall. I confess I hadn't noticed the child's name on it. Mr Crane wasn't sure when she would be out of hospital, I think his original plans were to send her home later."

"Forgive me," said Larry, intrigued, "but you don't sound like — well, like a foreigner. Surely I can detect a slight Devonshire accent?"

A grating laugh came through the twisted lips. "You have a sharp ear, Doctor. I was engaged to marry when I had this done to my face. I knew my fiancee would have insisted on marrying me in spite of everything, and I couldn't accept such a sacrifice. When I saw the slit eyes they had given me, I thought I looked like a Chinaman. So I became a Chinese cook. I'd always been interested in cooking. I wore this."

From a table at his side he took what appeared to be a chicken skin, or a child's balloon, and with a deft movement placed it over his face.

It transformed him at once, not to any semblance of good looks, Larry thought, but at least it covered those scars, and gave him a part-normal look.

"It was extremely uncomfortable to wear, especially in a hot kitchen," said Ah Soy, "but I had little choice. Either retire into my shell — I once considered becoming a monk; or try to make a new life for myself. Mr Crane was dining at the restaurant where I worked, and was especially pleased with a dish I had created. He found out my address, and came to see me. Then he offered me this job, and I jumped at it."

"But," said Larry, "all this paraphernalia — the goddess, forgive me, you appeared to be praying to when I entered."

The man laughed again. "When I heard you coming, I knelt down before my lady friend — to hide my face. I prefer the dim lighting, and Mr Crane furnished my quarters in the way he thought I might like. He doesn't know I'm not Chinese. It pleases me to keep up the image. I do smoke a little opium, as you probably detected from the scent, Doctor. I still get pain from my injuries, and it helps."

Larry gave a sympathetic nod.

"Will you help?" asked Larry. "You've had the experience of falling from a plane. Can you let all these people die without at least trying to help. Have either of the two stewardesses told you there's been a baby born since we started this trip? At least come and look at the controls man. There must be some common factor in all planes, surely?"

The man's eyes gleamed. "A wonderful man, Mr Crane. I owe him everything. For his little girl's sake, I'll try, though God knows what it will be like to feel the controls in my hands again, or whether I shall be capable of making the right decisions at the right time. What sort of terrain are we crossing now? The last time I looked out we were over the sea. A plane like this would sink in minutes."

"We're over what looks like a desert," said Larry, "Sand, I would think. It might be an advantage, offering a soft landing."

Still the man hesitated, then, "Do they all know of this? They seem pretty quiet out there."

"Most of them do," said Larry. "The stewardesses, a nurse, the baby's father, and two of the men. One other I have had to sedate, or he'd have frightened the others. The young mother hasn't been told, or the other ladies. We shall have to warn them at the last moment, of course. The main lights in the passenger lounge have been turned off, and they all have just a small light over their seats. I'm not sure whether we might be using precious fuel. Do you know anything about what it could be?"

"No, Mr Crane told me it would revolutionise the aircraft industry, but I have no idea what it might be. We can only hope it won't be too sensitive to shock and explode before we all have a chance to get out — even if I can get the plane down safely."

"By the way," said Larry, "I should like to know your real name — no one else will, I assure you."

"John Stanmore," he answered. "DFC."

"Thank you, John," said Larry. "I appreciate your confidence."

Picking up the rubber mask, John said "I'll wear this, and carry a tray through the aircraft. They may think I'm taking something up to the pilots. I can't promise anything, Doctor Groves, but I'm willing to try. We've probably overshot our target, and are flying over the dead heart of Australia, I would think. At least we won't be trying to land over a city. It makes things a little easier in some ways, though given a choice I'd feel a lot safer with a parachute."

"Just as well there aren't any," said Larry, "I can't imagine sending a mother and baby down in a parachute — and we have the pilot who's still unconscious. We must give him the same chance as the rest of us."

"Naturally, although carrying someone away in a stretcher will endanger the ones carrying it, if the plane should explode shortly after landing. If it does so on contact," he shrugged, "it will be quick. We shall be expected at the airport, naturally. They may even have started to look for us already. We must stay as close to the plane as possible after taking safety measures. They will see us better from the air."

Larry agreed. "I've had a look at what seems to be a communications system," he said, "but I'm no wireless boffin, and I'm afraid to touch anything."

John's thin shoulders, under the white coat he wore, lifted again, "Nor I, Doctor. The most we can do is hope and pray we may land somewhere without damaging the aircraft too much, or triggering off a fire, or explosion. What we must do is alert everybody so that as soon as we touch down they are all ready to get out at once. Impress on them they mustn't linger for *anything*. Just go for the escape chute and run. You noticed the chutes? One on either side of the passenger cabin, opened by a strong bar. There's a lever for each of them. They can't be opened by hand — in case of accidental knocks, presumably. Here are the levers, on the wall. The main danger, after we've landed is of fire." He touched his own face momentarily. "They must run like hell, as far away as they could manage, then throw themselves down on the ground as flat as possible, covering their heads with their hands."

"What about the young mother and her baby?" asked Larry, his mouth grim.

John nodded. "She will be ahead of all of us," he said, "You will see. Nowhere is the instinct to survive so great as in a mother with young."

"I expect you're right," said Larry.

"What about the pilot? We shall have to strap him to a stretcher. I'll hold one end, of course, but who to help me? You'll be in the cockpit, and we can't delay for long enough for you to get round."

John had already donned his rubber mask, and it was impossible to read anything from the smooth surface. "You must not be a stretcher-bearer, Doctor. Some of the others may be injured, and need your help. You must find two other men. Two who can be trusted not to panic and think only of their own safety. Men you can be sure of."

"My friend, Ken," said Larry, thoughtfully, "I know he'll be the first to volunteer. But who else? Mr Montgomery will be helping his wife and baby. Naturally, Sammy will be too woozy from the sedative I gave him, even if I thought he could be trusted to do it. It's out of the question to ask the girls. Asta will be looking after her charge, and the pilot's a heavy man, he'll need two men to carry him."

The very sound of Asta's name made Larry flinch. How was he going to control his natural instincts of protection for a girl he loved so much? An instinct as firmly planted in a man's nature as it had been when his remote forefather had fought tooth and claw to protect his mate. The most he would be able to do was see she got a fair chance to escape with little Vida, and not be pushed aside in the rush for freedom.

"I think the dark fellow, the Aborigine, for one end of the stretcher. He seems a sensible man, and a good strong one. Sammy must be given a good push and I'll try to see he gets away. The other two women, Mrs Murdoch and Mrs Munt, don't look hysterical types, but you never know. We shall see."

As the two men entered the plane's cockpit, Larry said "Would it be possible to jettison some supplies, John? First-Aid kit, water or tinned drinks, food. It may be some time before we're rescued, and the nights can be very cold. Blankets, that sort of thing. Get them out first, just before the plane lands, so that we can pick them up."

"Good thinking," said John, "only, they may land some way off. We'll need to be able to find them."

He was already sitting behind the controls, his hands moving about, testing, his eyes flickering from one dial to another. "There are some red plastic tops for the fridges in the kitchen," he said, "cut them into strips and tie one on to every piece you throw overboard. There's a small disposal hatch, where I throw out the rubbish. Use that. There's a good supply of tinned beer and lemonade. The cans should stand dropping. Tinned foods in the cupboards. When you've done that, tell everybody what's going to happen. Every minute is precious now — this fuel gauge is showing damned near empty. I'm going to switch off the automatic pilot now, and try to

252

get the feel of everything. You have about twenty minutes, I'd guess. I can't risk any longer. Make them all wrap up warm, in spite of the heat outside, but not enough to impede movement."

He nodded his head with its grotesque mask. Larry had the feeling that if anyone was going to be last aboard, it would be John Stanmore, DFC. There was a proud confidence in the set of those thin shoulders. The rubber mask was impatiently discarded, but somehow the exultant look on John's disfigured face transformed it. He was back again, in control.

He laid a hand momentarily on the pilot's arm, "Good luck, old chap," Larry said. "If anyone can get us down, you will, but if you don't — it was a pleasure to meet you."

There was a quick flicker of a smile, then, "Get going, Doc. Throw out everything you can lay your hands on, as quickly as possible. Get one of the girls to help you. They'll know where everything is. Don't forget a tin-opener."

Asta was in the kitchen when Larry ran in. She was making a hot drink for Vida.

"Drop everything," he said, "We're landing in just twenty minutes. Help me throw everything we can lay our hands on through this hatch. Mark it with a piece of red plastic if you can. Leave it if you can't. Drinks and first aid come first, then blankets."

Asta wasted no time in talking. Tearing the red plastic into strips with the aid of a pair of scissors from her pocket. Then hastily stuffing things through the hatch. "Do they all know?" she asked. "Mr Montgomery told me about the Chinese cook being a pilot. Is he going to be able to land us, Larry? Mrs Montgomery knows we're in trouble, though I doubt whether she realises how bad it is. She's already dressed, and the baby's well wrapped up. Her husband will do everything he can to get her out, of course."

"That only leaves Mrs Murdoch and Mrs Munt who don't know," said Larry. "You'd better go and prepare them now, hadn't you, my darling?"

He turned away to hide the flush in his cheeks at having called her what had slipped out so easily. Then he turned, and swept her into his arms. "Just in case this should be my last chance," he whispered, hoarsely, "one minute out of eternity. I love you, Asta." His kiss was fiercely passionate, burning her mouth, but her own passion matched his. Yet she pulled herself away. "We both have a job to do, Larry," she said, "there will be plenty of time later. I'll go and see about the passengers and warn Annie and Oggie. Little Vida is already dressed, and has her favourite Teddy tied on to her belt. She seems to think this is a replay of Action Man. I don't think this will come as a complete surprise to Mrs Murdoch, you know. She'll probably say she read it in the tea-leaves. Come to think of it, she *did*."

"No luggage," said Larry, "Time enough for that if we're lucky enough to land safely." Even as he spoke, there was a different sound to the engines, a spluttering. He gave one last look at Asta, then they both ran out to where the passengers were still in their seats, with Annie and Oggie moving about, answering questions, both as calm as though this was an everyday occurrence.

Asta nodded to Oggie, who bent over the two women, still knitting. There was a startled look from Mrs Munt, but Mrs Murdoch merely packed her needles and wool into a large coloured bag by her side, looking as composed as if her peeps into the future had already comforted her. Mrs Munt, her normal florid face pale, dropped her knitting on to the floor of the plane, getting out her rosary and passing it through her trembling hands.

"Fasten your seat-belts for the landing," said Larry, "but as soon as I call 'Now!' go as quickly as you can to one of the escape doors. There will be a canvas chute leading to the ground. Get down it as though the devil was after you. Then run. We may land perfectly safely. In fact, I have every confidence we will, but there is always the danger of the plane's catching fire, and you must get away until that danger's over. The stewardesses have already told you which order to go in, and whose help is needed. The best of luck to you all."

Annie standing over the still sleeping Sammy, shook him, then as a last resort, dashed a cup of water in his face. He awoke, spluttering, and regarded the scene with a blank stare.

"What did you do that for?" he demanded, angrily. Then as memory came flooding back, he caught the girl's sleeve in a terrified grasp. "We're going to crash, aren't we? Why did you wake me? Why didn't you let me go in my sleep?"

"We're not going to crash," came the unflurried reply, "At the worst it'll probably be only a bump on to the sand. But you must be ready to leave the plane at once, in case of fire. Get your coat on, Mr Salmon. I have other passengers to help. I'm going to put you in charge of one of the escape chutes, to see everyone gets off safely. I know I can rely on you."

A change came over the flabby face. Her diplomatic move worked. Sammy's chest grew by four inches, and he caught one of Annie's hands. This time she didn't pull away, merely smiled at him confidently.

"Thank you, Mr Salmon," she said, and swiftly leaned over and kissed him, "I know you won't let us down."

Mrs Montgomery and her baby had been brought into the main body of the plane, and her husband sat by them, his face white. Holding the baby in one arm, he held his wife's hand tightly. "Dear God," he was praying, "just give me five minutes to get them away. Just five minutes."

Asta had already taken her place beside Vida, ready to snatch the child up as soon as the plane touched down. Larry strapped himself into his old seat, where, by stretching out his hand, he could touch Asta's.

His eyes bored deeply into hers across that small gap. They told her of the depth of his love. Then her feet encountered something soft and yielding under her seat, and thinking it might be one of Vida's precious possessions, she undid her belt for a moment and felt for it. It wasn't until it was too late to push back that she realised they were the roses Dick had sent on to the plane when they left London. Specially packed in some water-retaining material, they looked as fresh as when she'd received them.

Against her will, Asta blushed and looked away, but not before Larry had seen them, and her embarrassed look. Uncontrolled tears came to her eyes as she saw the change that had come over Larry's face. The tenderness of a few minutes before had been replaced by a set mouth and jaw. The roses had told him Asta was not his. It reminded him that although she had responded to his kiss, there had been no answer to his "I love you, Asta." Steeling his heart, Larry looked straight in front of him, until, with a thud that made everyone's heart jump, the plane came to a halt.

10

ASTA stirred, hardly realising where she was. The narrow trench in the sand which Larry had scooped out for her and lined with a blanket had made a comfortable bed. Exhaustion had made her sleep right through the night, for they had all spent hours finding things that had been sprayed out of the aircraft before they landed, collecting firewood from some of the dead trees, and preparing for what might be a long wait before they were found.

Her first thought was for her small charge, but Vida was still fast asleep by her side, cuddling her beloved Teddy. Asta's own sleep had been filled with rapidly moving scenes, scenes where there was just one common factor — Larry.

Larry, standing outside the old house

in Mortimer Road, hands in pockets, and the sun turning his dark red hair to flame. Larry, gowned and masked working in the theatre of St Margaret's. Larry with his arms around her at Mummy's wedding, making her very soul vibrate as he kissed her.

Daylight followed quickly on dawn. The sky was of breath-taking beauty by now; cerulean blue, graduating to a pale nile green on the horizon. Apart from the sky, however, there was little beauty in the landscape that surrounded them. Here and there a dead, stark gum tree, lifting its arms to pray for the water that hardly ever fell. Mile after mile of reddish sand and rocks, and over it all, a deathly hush. No 'Dawn chorus' here, she thought; even the birds have deserted it.

The men had made a large bonfire, not just for comfort, Larry had told her, but in case of any aircraft going over. She just vaguely remembered feeling Larry tuck them both up, and his saying "I'm on first watch. If you need anything in the night, I'll only be a few yards away."

There had been the lusty cries of tiny Jamie, hastily soothed in his mother's arms, then sleep.

Turning, and resting on one elbow, Asta saw that Larry had made his own bed only a few feet away. One of his hands, relaxed in sleep had been thrown out over the sands and was almost touching hers. She studied the face so near her own. There was a fair stubble of beard on his chin and upper lips. It looked soft, she thought, and longed to touch it with her hands. It was the same colour as a thick mat of hair on his half-exposed chest. As she watched, a tender little smile lurked on the corners of his lips. "He must be dreaming of something nice," she told herself, "If only it could be me."

The intense silence was only broken by a faint crackling from the fire, beside which the Aborigine sat, legs crossed, gazing into the flames.

It was almost a relief when Vida

stirred, and called out "Has my Daddy come yet, Asta? He's an awful long time finding us, isn't he?" She sat up, rubbing her eyes fretfully. "I don't like it here very much, do you, Asta? Will it be as hot as it was yesterday?"

"I hope not," said Asta, soothingly, "come on, let's get you dressed, shall we?"

Other humps in the sand were stirring now. Putting her finger to her lips, Asta said, "Don't disturb Doctor Larry yet, he's been on watch."

At the sound of her voice, however, Larry was up, scratching the stubble on his face. "What wouldn't I do for a razor," he said. "I feel like one of the wild men of Borneo."

"I don't suppose any of us feel at our best," she said, with a little grimace. "I do have a comb, if you'd like to borrow it."

"Thanks," he said, taking it from her. "We have a saying in Australia, 'you have to be pretty good mates to share a comb.'"

264

Seeing it on the sand beside her, Asta hastily stowed away the diary she'd left there. It had been on the seat when they evacuated the plane, and after she'd donned the thick olive-green anorak, she'd thrust it into a large map pocket in front, together with a bag of fruit drops for Vida, and a big supply of tissues.

Asta had spent the last hour before going to sleep getting her diary up to date.

'We're all safely out of the plane [she'd written], except for the pilot and Sammy. Larry has told me about him. He wasn't Chinese at all but a bomber pilot in the last war. He must have stayed in the cockpit of our plane, perhaps trying to put out the fire.

'The first explosion came about ten minutes after we all got out and had run as far away as we could. Larry carried Vida, and after I'd tripped over something in the sand, very nearly carried me too. My arm still aches from the way he dragged me along.

'After he'd thrown us both down on the sand behind the shelter of what I think is an ant-hill, he went back and helped some of the others to safety. The Mortimers are near me now, both mother and baby seem fine. Oggie and Annie helped get the two other women to shelter.

'I feel really dreadful about Sammy. He lost his life trying to get as much of our luggage out as possible. He kept hurling it out of the plane as far away as possible, and Homer pulled a lot of it to safety, until Larry stopped him, and made him take cover. A lot of our things were saved, but no one would have thought it worth the poor man's life. Larry kept shouting to him to leave the plane, but he didn't seem to hear. Larry had just started to run towards the plane when it exploded. I hardly dared open my eyes for some seconds, but when I did, he was on his feet again, and running towards Sammy, who'd been blown right out of the doorway. I could see he was dead, even from where I was. Ken ran after Larry, and giving him a rugby tackle, forced him down. None too soon, for a second explosion totally wrecked the plane.

'It was a ghastly sight. Within a few minutes the plane was just a sort of red-hot tangle. I keep thinking of that brave pilot, and wondering whether he *wanted* to die?

'Ken said that perhaps Sammy was still under the influence of the sedative Larry gave him, but I prefer to think he was ashamed of his conduct earlier, and wanted to make some amends.

'There is some hope that the pilot, John Stanmore, may have been sending out 'May-Day' signals, giving our position, but Larry says he'd already told him he knew nothing about radio. Still, they are bound to be looking out for us. The general feeling amongst us all is that of optimism. We'd even be cheerful if it wasn't for the loss of those two brave men.

'Vida is as bright as ever, quite certain that Daddy will come over the sand in his Rolls. Fortunately her teddy-bear survived the ordeal, one of his legs got slightly torn, but I had a needle and cotton in my small case, rescued by Sammy, so I repaired him and put a bandage on the place. Vida loves him all the more for his honourable scars.

'Mrs Montgomery seems to have come to no harm, and is feeding the baby, who sleeps peacefully most of the time. He is a source of great entertainment for Vida, who hasn't quite worked out how he came to be on the plane at all, but thinks it's a good idea on the Montgomery's part. She has the self-imposed task of laying out the squares of torn-up towels and sheets we've managed to salvage and are using for nappies. We can't wash them, of course. We must have every drop of liquid we have for drinking. Anyway, little Jamie's posterior is still pink and firm.

'Homer has just gone off into the desert to look for more of the things we jettisoned from the plane. Some of them must be scattered for miles. He's a wonderful asset to us, coming as he does from a race that has coped with this sort of terrain for generations. He doesn't seem to even feel the sun on his head. Larry says some of the stuff is at least ten miles away, and he'd never have dared to let anyone but Homer go, for fear of getting lost. Fortunately one of the things Sammy pitched out of the plane before it blew up was a sort of haversack, which turned out to be a collapsible canoe. "Not much good to us, in the desert someone said," but Ken pounced on it at once. With the aid of a few branches of dead wood, and some of the blankets that were salvaged, he soon built us a shelter, under the ant-hill, in the shade. The canoe is very comfortable to sit in, with its pneumatic sides, and I'm particularly glad to have it for Mrs Montgomery's sake. The sun, after — about nine o'clock, is terribly hot, though Homer says this is the 'cool' season.

'Larry has taken charge, and is working out a system of rationing. Homer had just come back from one of his 'walk-abouts' with a broad beam on his face. He's found a small waterhole, a 'billabong' he calls it. It's only about a mile away. We thought at first of moving everything to be near the water, but Larry thinks we should stay by the burnt-out plane, as that will be more visible when they come to rescue us. Still, at least we won't die of thirst. The men are rigging up some sort of sledge, from bits of metal that came from the plane, and will carry water every morning. We shall be able to wash Jamie's nappies now. That's a blessing.

'Ken has rigged up some sort of punkah, like they use in India, and put it over the baby's cot, made from another cardboard box and a blanket. It's to be hoped little Jamie won't grow up with an inferiority complex, sleeping in one cardboard box after another. We take it in turns to pull the string (somebody's pyjama cord) and keep the flies at bay. They are a particularly horrible species, with a sort of grey arrow on their backs. Ugh!

'Little Jamie's father, together with the two other women passengers, Mrs Murdoch and Mrs Munt, are out gathering large bits of wood to make an 'SOS' on the sand. I'd have thought the wreck of the plane would have been enough, but it gives them something to do, I suppose.

'Those two women are terrific. You'd think they'd lived on a desert island all their lives. They even managed to save their knitting. At least, it looks the same wool, but they've unravelled what they were making, and are now busily knitting little vests for Jamie, one red and one green. Poor Jamie's layette went up with the plane, and he's wearing the oddest assortment of articles donated by those who had some of their baggage saved.

'Larry and I have hardly exchanged more than a few words since the disaster. We've both been very busy, of course. Last night, we were all sitting round a huge bonfire the men had built, Ken sitting next to me with little Vida between his knees. His voice sounded almost unearthly as he sang to her. Strangely, the first bird I've heard since we came here joined in. Ken sang an old love song I've heard mother sing. 'All through the night there's a little brown bird singing, singing songs of love in the darkness and the dew.' I was glad we were only in the light of the fire, for the tears would keep falling down my cheeks however hard I swallowed.

'Why was Larry sitting on the other side of the fire, when he could have joined me here? I keep remembering the way he kissed me when we both thought we might be going to die at any moment?

'Surely he must have meant it. I feel certain he did. I wondered if it was just to distract me from the danger, but I can't believe it was. I *won't* believe it was, but what can I do?

'Could it be those beastly roses Dick sent me? Larry doesn't strike me as the jealous type. Why didn't I tell him then, that I love him with all my heart? What made me break away so suddenly?

'Another minute or two would have made no difference. The words just didn't come in time — but surely he must have felt my love for him? It surely can't be possible for a man to be so blind.

'*Later*. We're all trying to pretend it's only a matter of hours before someone comes to our rescue, but I'm worried about the baby, and little Vida. It's so terribly hot, and the flies seem to have found us and come from miles around to torment.

'I've been so absorbed in my own affairs I hadn't noticed until now, but I think Ken is falling in love with Annie. He follows her around with his eyes, and she seeks his company too. They'd make such a splendid couple. I saw them go for water to the billabong this morning, and they were hand in hand. I do hope it works out for them — if we're rescued. But of course we shall be, it's morbid to think of anything else.

'I could get up and join Larry over there, but he's talking to Mrs Murdoch, holding up that ridiculous green vest, and laughing. I don't know what to say to him, anyway,

I still have my stupid pride, but if I lose Larry I shall wish we had died in this awful place. Nothing in the world matters to me so much as working with him, loving him, bearing his children.

'I often watch Flora Montgomery with little Jamie in her arms, and it makes me ache with longing for a child of my own, a red-headed son, like his father. Even seeing Larry at a distance makes my heart pound, and I long for him to come over and put his arms around me, in front of them all.

'My biro is starting to run out, so this may be the last entry I shall be able to make.'

* * *

Ken Markham, just back from a walk in the fast-gathering dusk pulled Annie down to sit with him, beside Asta. Poking the glowing fire with a piece of metal, he said "We want you to be

275

the first to know, Asta, Annie and I are engaged." He caught Annie's hand, and exhibited a gold signet ring that had been on his own little finger. "Wish us luck, Asta," he said. "If there had been a parson among us, we'd have made him marry us on the spot, wouldn't we, sweetheart?"

Asta smiled at his enthusiasm, but could hardly stifle a pang of envy. Was her own disappointment making her pretty-minded? she wondered, then giving herself a little mental shake, she said "What wonderful news, Annie, I hope you and Ken will be marvellously happy."

"I shall be a lot happier when I can get a shave," said Ken, fingering his black stubble. "Seems we all used electric razors. Still," he laughed, "if Annie can accept me like this, she must love me, eh?" He caught Annie in his arms and kissed her firmly.

"I shall have to ration your kisses until you either shave that off or grow a decent beard," said Annie, kissing him again, in case he thought she meant it.

"Old Larry's beard grows quickly," said Ken, "it's quite respectable already. Makes him look like an ancient Roman, doesn't it?"

Little Vida was beginning to get cross and restless. This new game was beginning to pall now that all her favourite toys, with the exception of Teddy, had gone up in flames. She was even exhausting everyone's stock of stories. The carefully hoarded bag of fruit drops Asta had saved was finished.

It was early in the morning, and quite cool when Vida awoke, and sat up in her blanket bed. Yesterday, Doctor Larry had given her a 'flying angel' on his shoulders to the billabong. It would be nice to go there again, and paddle in the water.

Larry was sitting by the fire, on guard, when she went over to him. "Take me to the water again, Doctor Larry," she demanded, imperiously. "I want to swim."

"I can't take you just now, poppet," said Larry, weary from loss of sleep, "I have rather a lot to do. Perhaps this evening, eh?"

Vida pouted. "Daddy would have taken me, if he was here. I think you're mean, so there." Stamping her foot, she turned away. Keeping a wary eye on the still sleeping people, she started out alone. Perhaps if Doctor Larry saw her going he'd change his mind. Larry was too deep in thought to notice her quiet footsteps, however, and nobody else stirred. That nice Uncle Ken's place was empty, so maybe he was already at the water-hole, drawing the water for the day. She was sure she could walk that far, and Uncle Ken would pull her back on the sled, as he had done before.

He'd be glad to see her, Vida felt sure. The thought of a lovely paddle in the cool water, shaded by gum trees and full of chattering cockatoos was a spur, making her forget her feet. Although they had healed nicely after the operation, they were apt to ache a little still, and Asta had been massaging them night and morning.

She set off, slowly at first, not to attract attention, then hurrying as fast as she could over the sand. The track seemed a lot longer than it had before, and the sun was getting up, making a haze over the horizon, shimmering on the sand, and making her eyes ache.

Propping Teddy up on a small rock she told him, "You stay there 'til I come back. You're awful heavy, and your fur's hot. I'll get you when I've had my paddle. You just stay there, I won't be long."

Trudging on, she began to waver. The billabong was nowhere in sight, so maybe it would be better to go back, after all, and let Doctor Larry bring her later.

Impatiently she pushed the damp red-gold curls from her eyes, and hit out at the clustering flies that were starting to torment her. Asta had been covering her arms and legs, and the baby's too, with some fly-repellant cream she had in her bag, but the effect had worn off by now, and the flies enticed by the beads of perspiration on the child's face got bolder every minute.

Covering her face with her hands, Vida ran and ran until she was finally slowed down by the pain in her feet. Although she wailed loudly for Asta, her voice was lost in the vast silence around her. Seeing some shade under a large rock, she staggered to it, covering her face from the flies with her dress. Asta would come and find her soon, she felt sure, or else Doctor Larry.

Lying with one ear to the ground, Vida heard a cool, rustling sound near her head. Then something slithered by her side, and peering from under her cover, she saw a brightly hued snake, with black beady eyes, regarding her with interest. She was so petrified with fear that she couldn't move, and the snake, deciding she was harmless, slid away out of sight.

Daddy had often told her that if ever she was lost, she must stay still, and he'd come and fetch her. She curled up again, drowsy with the heat, and ate a small apple she'd put in her pocket against emergencies.

She'd been there for two hours or more before Asta and Larry found her. Asta held Teddy in her arms. They'd found him on the way. Clutching Vida in her arms, Asta was almost in tears as she scolded the child with relief.

"I'm thirsty, Asta," she wailed, "and a nasty snake nearly bit me." Asta had brought a small plastic bottle of water with her, which Vida drank from, greedily.

"We thought you must have gone to the billabong, and been drowned," said Larry, sternly, "Don't ever wander off like that again, will you?"

Larry couldn't look stern for long, however, and he gave her a smile as he leaned over and picked her up in his arms.

"Has my Daddy come on a train?"

asked Vida. "I thought he'd bring his car for me."

"On a train?" asked Larry "That's an odd notion, young lady. I don't think they have many stations around these parts."

"I heard a train," persisted Vida, "Just over there, it sounded a long way off, but I heard it whistle."

"I expect you were dreaming, dear," said Asta, "maybe it was one of those noisy cockatoos screeching. There aren't any trains around here, I'm afraid." Then her expression changed.

"It's a funny thing though, Larry, just as I was going off to sleep last night, I thought *I* heard a train whistle, too. You know how quiet it is at night. Cockatoos don't fly around at night, do they? I thought I must have imagined it, but it's so strange Vida should think the same, isn't it?"

"Which direction?" asked Larry. "You're right, it *is* too much of a coincidence. There *is* a railway line going across Australia, you know, much of it over desert country. As soon as I get you both back to camp, I'll get Homer to come and find out whether we could be near the track. If we are, we'll stay by it until a train comes through, and stop it."

Asta put a hand on one of his bare brown arms. "Larry, please. Don't go off into that awful desert, you could get lost, or be overcome by the heat."

"I must," he answered, "it may be our only chance. There's always the possibility they may not find us in time, and the food won't last much longer."

"Then let me go with you," she said, eagerly, "I'm a very good walker, all nurses are." Her eyes were alight, and no man in his senses could fail to see the love in them.

He stopped by a big flat rock, Vida, tired out by her adventure, asleep in his arms.

"I told you on the plane," he said, softly. "I love you, Asta, but unless you're willing to spend the rest of your life with me, I'd rather give you up — now, before I got used to being with you. I know you were engaged to be married before, and I can't believe, or perhaps I'm afraid to hope, that you've really broken it off for good. Dick doesn't seem to think so, does he? I couldn't help noticing the roses he sent you — " His voice broke, and he gazed into the distance, his eyes clouded.

"You never met Dick," she said, "Only saw him once or twice. He is a very attractive man, and I'll admit I thought I loved him enough to marry. But now I know my feelings were not strong enough for a man I had wanted to call my husband. Dick had some very good points, and I should have never let it go as far as it did. I was to blame for that entirely. Yet, without being unkind, I know that Dick will recover as soon as he faces the fact of my refusal."

Facing him, she said, "It was never like the love I feel for you, my darling.

I shall never change again, I promise you. This is for keeps."

Across the sleeping child, she leaned over, and their lips met in a long kiss.

"Your beard tickles," she laughed, "but I love it — please keep it, will you, Larry?"

After a rest, Homer and Larry set off in a brilliant moonlight, carrying a torch rescued from someone's baggage. Larry had no fear of getting lost while Homer was with him. Homer Pidgeon was aptly named. He seemed to have inherited a built-in compass from his Aborigine ancestors.

About three miles out into the desert, he stopped and sniffed the air. "They were right," he said. "A train has passed near here, I can smell it." His wide nostrils flared. "Yes, the smell of fuel, and hot metal."

Half a mile further on, and they could see the silver snake of a railway track in the moonlight.

"I don't suppose many trains go by,"

said Larry, "one of us had better go back to the camp and tell the others. It had better be you, Homer." he laughed, the relief of their discovery in his voice. "Well done, we'd never have managed without you. I'd only lose my way if I go, and become another casualty. If I hear a train coming, I'll stand by the rails and flash an SOS with the torch. Even if the driver doesn't stop, he'll probably see it, and report." Back at the camp, Asta spent a worrying time until Homer came running back with the swift easy lope of a native, beaming the good news to them all. She wasn't too happy at the idea of Larry being out there keeping vigil on his own, but Homer assured her there were no dangerous wild animals in those parts, and at least now there were hopes of a speedy delivery from the camp, becoming more odious every day.

Sooner than they had thought possible, the quiet was shattered by the noise of a helicopter, which hovered over them, and then landed a few yards away.

Vida went running across the sand to her father, who swept her up in his arms, his face puckered with emotion and relief.

Looking across Vida's curls he said "Thank you, thank you, my dear, for looking after my girl. There are two Land-Rovers on the way, should be here within the hour. My God! I thought you must have all died in the crash. They started to get a message on the radio, then there was a terrible noise, and silence."

Larry jumped out of the helicopter and, in a second, Asta was in his arms, being held so tightly against his chest she could hardly breathe. Then her hands were touching the roughness of his face as she struggled to keep back the tears of relief.

The harsh landscape around them now seemed superbly beautiful, a backcloth for the *Desert Song*. She was with him for always — for ever and ever.

★ ★ ★

'Dear Diary,

So much to fill in, it's weeks since I wrote anything. I'm so wonderfully happy — Larry and I were married a week ago.

'He has had the offer of a partnership in Sydney, and we are going to make our home here.

'Mr Crane insisted on giving us the lease of a lovely bungalow near Manly, in exchange (he says) for having Vida for holidays. I know it's just an excuse, in case we refused the house as an outright gift.

'Jamie and Flora came to see us, the baby is absolutely wonderful — the image of his father. Larry agrees with me that we should start a family of our own as soon as possible.

'Mummy and Jim flew over for the wedding — another present from Mr Crane — incredible man. Mrs Murdoch and Mrs Munt came, too. They passed broad hints that if I ever want any knitting done — Only no green and red vests for *my* children, please!

'Ken and Annie are getting married next month. He made his debut at the Sydney Opera House — and was a wonderful success, booked up for a year ahead.

'Oggie has transferred to another air-line, but sent us a beautiful wedding present, and promises to call on us every time she comes to Australia.

'We invited Homer, of course, but he didn't come to the wedding. We would like to have seen him. If he hadn't found that billabong — and then the railway — we might all have died out there in that arid place.

'We often speak of 'Sammy', who seemed such a coward at first, then gave his life just to save our belongings. That brave man the pilot, too. I can see Larry coming up the path. Being married to him is the most wonderful thing.'

WITH SOMEBODY ELSE
Theresa Charles

Rosamond sets off for Cornwall with Hugo to meet his family, blissfully unaware of the shocks in store for her.

A SUMMER FOR STRANGERS
Claire Hamilton

Because she had lost her job, her flat and she had no money, Tabitha agreed to pose as Adam's future wife although she believed the scheme to be deceitful and cruel.

VILLA OF SINGING WATER
Angela Petron

The disquieting incidents that occurred at the Vatican and the Colosseum did not trouble Jan at first, but then they became increasingly unpleasant and alarming.

DOCTOR NAPIER'S NURSE
Pauline Ash

When cousins Midge and Derry are entered as probationer nurses on the same day but at different hospitals they agree to exchange identities.

A GIRL LIKE JULIE
Louise Ellis

Caroline absolutely adored Hugh Barrington, but then Julie Crane came into their lives. Julie was the kind of girl who attracts men without even trying.

COUNTRY DOCTOR
Paula Lindsay

When Evan Richmond bought a practice in a remote country village he did not realise that a casual encounter would lead to the loss of his heart.

ENCORE
Helga Moray

Craig and Janet realise that their true happiness lies with each other, but it is only under traumatic circumstances that they can be reunited.

NICOLETTE
Ivy Preston

When Grant Alston came back into her life, Nicolette was faced with a dilemma. Should she follow the path of duty or the path of love?

THE GOLDEN PUMA
Margaret Way

Catherine's time was spent looking after her father's Queensland farm. But what life was there without David, who wasn't interested in her?

HOSPITAL BY THE LAKE
Anne Durham

Nurse Marguerite Ingleby was always ready to become personally involved with her patients, to the despair of Brian Field, the Senior Surgical Registrar, who loved her.

VALLEY OF CONFLICT
David Farrell

Isolated in a hostel in the French Alps, Ann Russell sees her fiancé being seduced by a young girl. Then comes the avalanche that imperils their lives.

NURSE'S CHOICE
Peggy Gaddis

A proposal of marriage from the incredibly handsome and wealthy Reagan was enough to upset any girl — and Brooke Martin was no exception.

A DANGEROUS MAN
Anne Goring

Photographer Polly Burton was on safari in Mombasa when she met enigmatic Leon Hammond. But unpredictability was the name of the game where Leon was concerned.

PRECIOUS INHERITANCE
Joan Moules

Karen's new life working for an authoress took her from Sussex to a foreign airstrip and a kidnapping; to a real life adventure as gripping as any in the books she typed.

VISION OF LOVE
Grace Richmond

When Kathy takes over the rundown country kennels she finds Alec Stinton, a local vet, very helpful. But their friendship arouses bitter jealousy and a tragedy seems inevitable.

CRUSADING NURSE
Jane Converse

It was handsome Dr. Corbett who opened Nurse Susan Leighton's eyes and who set her off on a lonely crusade against some powerful enemies and a shattering struggle against the man she loved.

WILD ENCHANTMENT
Christina Green

Rowan's agreeable new boss had a dream of creating a famous perfume using her precious Silverstar, but Rowan's plans were very different.

DESERT ROMANCE
Irene Ord

Sally agrees to take her sister Pam's place as La Chartreuse the dancer, but she finds out there is more to it than dyeing her hair red and looking like her sister.

HEART OF ICE
Marie Sidney

How was January to know that not only would the warmth of the Swiss people thaw out her frozen heart, but that she too would play her part in helping someone to live again?

LUCKY IN LOVE
Margaret Wood

Companion-secretary to wealthy gambler Laura Duxford, who lived in Monaco, seemed to Melanie a fabulous job. Especially as Melanie had already lost her heart to Laura's son, Julian.

NURSE TO PRINCESS JASMINE
Lilian Woodward

Nick's surgeon brother, Tom, performs an operation on an Arabian princess, and she invites Tom, Nick and his fiancé to Omander, where a web of deceit and intrigue closes about them.

THE WAYWARD HEART
Eileen Barry

Disaster-prone Katherine's nickname was "Kate Calamity", but her boss went too far with an outrageous proposal, which because of her latest disaster, she could not refuse.

FOUR WEEKS IN WINTER
Jane Donnelly

Tessa wasn't looking forward to meeting Paul Mellor again — she had made a fool of herself over him once before. But was Orme Jared's solution to her problem likely to be the right one?

SURGERY BY THE SEA
Sheila Douglas

Medical student Meg hadn't really wanted to go and work with a G.P. on the Welsh coast although the job had its compensations. But Owen Roberts was certainly not one of them!